RUMORS, TALES, WHISPERS & WONDERS

LEGENDS OF GROWING UP A SMALL TOWN NOBODY

inkblotz press

RUMORS, TALES, WHISPERS & WONDERS

Legends of Growing Up a Small Town Nobody

A Second Collection of Short Stories by Mariano Velez

Publisher: Mariano Velez, Inkblotz Press

Cover design and layout by: Mariano Velez III - M3 Arts
Interior illustrations by: Mariano Velez III - M3 Arts

First Edition: March 29, 2026
ISBN: 979-8-9947151-0-9

Printed in the United States of America

For more information, more stories, and a bit more mischief, visit: xinkblotz.com

Dedication

For the afternoons that smelled like tortillas and sun,
for the games that ended only when the day demanded it,
and for the mischief that made every corner of Calexico feel like home.

For the voices that laughed, yelled, and sometimes argued—
the friends, the siblings, the neighbors—
whose small adventures became big stories.

For my family—
who gave me the stories, the humor,
and the quiet courage to chase them down
before they disappeared into memory.

And for Calexico and Mexicali,
where every rumor, tale, whisper, and wonder
was worth catching, keeping, and passing along.

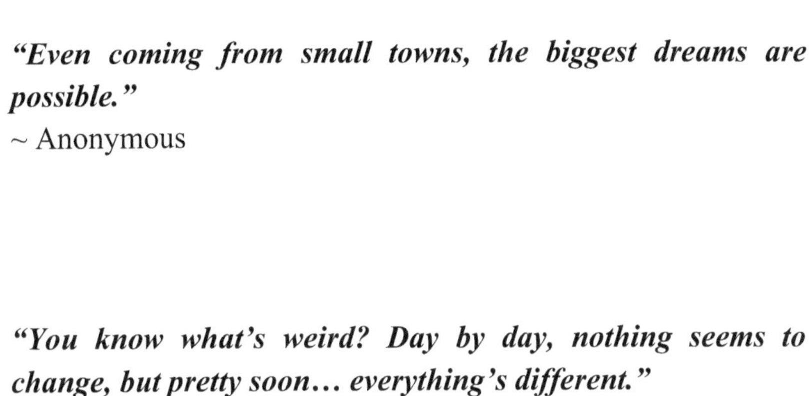

"Even coming from small towns, the biggest dreams are possible."

~ Anonymous

"You know what's weird? Day by day, nothing seems to change, but pretty soon… everything's different."

~ Bill Watterson

"Laughter is timeless, imagination has no age, dreams are forever."

~ Walt Disney

Foreword: On Legends and Memory

All stories begin somewhere, but few remain the same once they leave our mouths.

What started as mischief, a small triumph, a backyard experiment, or a summer afternoon in a corner of Calexico has, over time, grown into something larger—something taller, wilder, and a little more impossible than the day it happened.

Every legend starts small. Sometimes it's a prank, a scrape, a daring stunt, or just a hot afternoon begging for something extraordinary.

But legends, as you'll discover, have a way of growing. They stretch, wobble, and get louder and stranger with every telling.

These stories, grounded in actual events, are like that: at once true and exaggerated, personal and universal, small yet expansive.

They are drawn from lived moments and real experiences, shaped by memory and time.

They are legends—not of knights and dragons, but of ordinary lives magnified by memory, curiosity, and the inevitable embellishments of retelling.

Each telling adds color; each listener adds weight.

Laughter and sighs transform the everyday into something mythic.

You may notice moments that seem a little too wild, a little too perfect, a little too funny to be entirely true.

They are.

And yet, in every exaggeration, every tall tale, there is a kernel of truth:

> *~the feel of a sunbaked street, the echo of laughter off a neighbor's wall,*
>
> *~the smell of tortillas in the morning,*
>
> *~the thrill of discovering something new before the rest of the world caught on.*

These are the stories we tell to remember who we were, who we are, and what it felt like to be alive in a particular place and time.

They are the legends of our family, our neighborhood, our summers. Small miracles dressed in the familiar.

And now, they are yours to wander through, to smile at, to shake your head at, and perhaps, to pass on.

Step carefully, but step in.

Expect to stumble over wild ideas, laugh at impossible feats, and shake your head at the sheer audacity of it all.

These are stories of growing up, of curiosity, of mischief, and of the stubborn joy of being alive.

Like any good legend, they are best enjoyed with a smile, a sense of wonder, and the occasional disbelief that yes… somehow, it all really happened.

Because that is how legends work.

They grow.

They change.

They live.

And the more you tell them, the more alive they become.

Table of Contents

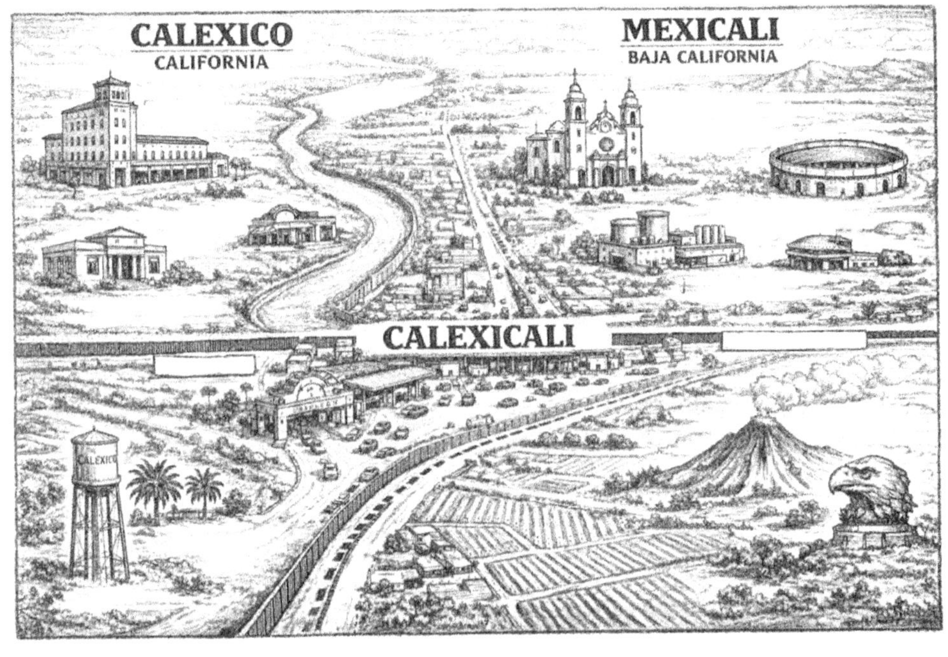
CALEXICO
CALIFORNIA
MEXICALI
BAJA CALIFORNIA
CALEXICALI
CALEXICO

Calexicali

Living life in two cultures is like having two lunchboxes—one full of tacos and the other full of peanut butter sandwiches—and trying not to mix them up in front of your friends.

On one side of the border, recess is running barefoot across asphalt so hot it can fry a tortilla, dodging soccer balls, bikes, and that one dog that thinks everyone is fair game.

On the other side, it's hopscotch, dodgeball, and the mysterious stickiness of cafeteria floors.

Even everyday stuff gets a makeover. A corner store can mean fresh bolillos and sweet tamarind candies in one town, and chips and soda in the other.

Your jokes are like currency—you tell one in Spanish and everyone laughs; tell it in English, and you get a blank stare, or worse, a polite "ha."

Families are the same, but not. One side says, "Lávate las manos, siéntate y comé." The other says, "Finish your homework before dessert." Somehow, you're left translating life like a tiny, overworked UN interpreter.

And in the middle of it all, you figure out a flavor all your own—a little sweet, a little spicy, and completely your own. Two lunchboxes, one kid, endless stories.

That's life in Calexico. And Mexicali. For those of us with roots on both sides of the border, though we never say it, it's *Calexicali.*

The language here is its own kind of magic—and its own kind of puzzle. Mexicali Spanish can be formal and precise, or rough and full of slang so wild that outsiders wouldn't have a clue what anyone's saying.

Some words don't exist anywhere else; some are made up on the spot, understood only by those who grew up here. *If you know, you know.*

Cross the border into Calexico, and Spanglish rules the day. It's everywhere: at the bus stop, in classrooms, on the corner with the tienda clerk.

Sure, Spanglish exists in other Latino communities, but here it's different—it has a rhythm, a cadence, a stubborn refusal to fit neatly into English or Spanish.

Living here means learning to speak in the pauses, the borrowed words, the laughter between languages.

It's lively, unpredictable, and completely, unmistakably ours.

Growing up in Calexico, visits across the border were a regular thing. They could happen any day of the week, often unplanned: a haircut, a dental appointment, a quick stop at la pharmacia, or simply to grab a meal.

We never thought of it this way back then, but crossing the border—walking past the turnstiles and into that wash of heat, dust, and the chaotic symphony of shouting vendors, clattering carts, and the occasional bark of a street dog—meant traveling into another nation.

International travel.

Fancy, grown-up, expensive. For us, it was casual. We were just going for food, for family, for the little things that made sense on both sides of the line.

Most Saturdays in Mexicali were adventures wrapped in errands. We went for necessities—ingredients for the weekend carne asada, a fresh haircut, maybe a trinket to brighten a shelf—but the city itself was the reward.

Just after crossing, we'd pull into a plazita, the air thick with smells: freshly fried churros, roasting meat, sweet aguas frescas, and the faint metallic tang of coins jingling on counters.

Vendors shouted greetings, displaying hand-woven zarapes, carved Aztec calendars, soft leather sandals. Each stall was a treasure chest; every corner a new surprise.

On the east corner stood Zapatería Tres Hermanos. Its twin entrances spilled the rich scent of polished leather, mingling with faint hints of shoe polish, sweat, and warm dust—the kind that makes you wrinkle your nose and grin at the same time.

Behind it, the peletería hummed quietly with its own life. Boots and belts were shaped by hands that knew every curve and crease, and the smell of freshly tooled leather drifted out in waves, mingling with the sun, the dust, and the distant sizzle of street food. I would pause for a moment and breathe it all in—sharp, warm, unmistakable, an experience all its own.

A few steps farther, the flauta shop beckoned. Tomato sauce bubbled, tortillas crisped, oil hissed and spat little sparks of steam. I remember the way my stomach would twist in anticipation.

One visit with Mom, Dad, my brother, and sisters, the place was packed. Ranchera music blared from a rickety radio perched on the counter. Jugs of aguas frescas—jamaica, horchata, limón, piña—lined the counter, glinting in the morning light. Waiters darted between tables, collecting orders and delivering steaming plates.

"¿Cuántas quiere, oiga?"

"Dame tres docenas. Y una pata curtida."

"¿Y de tomar?"

"Una horchata, una jamaica, cuatro Cokas."

A few minutes later, cold drinks clinked onto the table, and piping-hot flautas arrived, smothered in spicy tomato sauce and crowned with shredded cabbage. The aroma alone could make a kid forget his own name.

Then the single funniest thing happened—at least, my siblings thought so.

After polishing off my flautas and chugging the last of my soda, I reared back and let out a belch like no other—loud, resonant, almost capable of shaking my fillings loose.

The room went dead silent. Only the gentle bubbling of oil could be heard.

Someone shouted, "¡Cochino!"

I nearly toppled off my seat, laughing so hard my stomach hurt. My brother and sisters laughed too, though I think my brother may have been blamed.

And just like that, the chaos of the morning—food, family, music, and mischief—felt like pure magic.

Keep walking, and you'd enter a corridor of candy stores stretching along the sidewalks, piñatas swinging in impossible shapes—superheroes frozen mid-leap, animals with wide painted eyes, stars so bright they made your vision dance. Inside, shelves and bins overflowed with Mexican sweets of every color and texture: chewy, crunchy, sticky, sugary.

For any kid with a few pesos, it was paradise.

A little farther on, Plaza Mariachi revealed itself like a hidden stage tucked between the streets. This was where the mariachis gathered, waiting to be hired by anyone looking for a full band, a trio, or just a lone singer with a big voice.

Musicians tuned guitars and violins, the sharp twang mingling with laughter and drifting conversation. Some strummed quietly, warming up their fingers; others riffed freely, their notes spiraling into the warm evening air, tangling with the smell of roasted corn, leather belts, and sun-warmed pavement.

Every so often a car would ease up to the curb and someone would lean out the window to say, "*Ocupo un mariachi pa' un cumpleaños.*"

Instantly, a handful of musicians—charro suits gleaming even in the fading light—would break from the shade and stroll over, instruments in hand, ready to turn any occasion into a moment worth remembering.

Panaderías filled the gaps between shops, sending up ribbons of sugar and yeast—conchas dusted with sugar crystals, golden birotes still warm from the oven.

Sunlight glinted off the cobblestones, and a gentle breeze carried the mingled scents of baked goods, leather, and sizzling street food.

Every sense came alive.

Every step made you feel part of a city vibrating with sound, color, and life.

Downhill, La Yarda unfurled like a living mosaic. Wooden crates groaned under piles of oranges, melons, cilantro, and tomatoes, their colors blazing in the sunlight. Vendors shouted their prices over the hum of the crowd, voices weaving through the clatter of baskets and the shuffle of feet.

Dust rose from the sunbaked ground, mingling with the sharp sweetness of citrus, the green tang of herbs, and the faint, nutty aroma of spilled grain—earthy, warm, alive.

And then, there it was: the taco stand. *Tacos Tormentas del Desierto*—or at least that's what I remember it being called. A six-by-six grill, a simple counter wrapping two sides, a roof with walls everywhere but the entrance. Four men moved like a well-rehearsed dance, ladling, flipping, slicing, and garnishing with effortless rhythm.

One older gentleman, sporting a cowboy hat, manned the register with a chrome-plated .357 tucked into his belt, slicing avocados for patrons.

Every bite was perfect—warm, spicy, layered with flavors that made your taste buds tingle. Every time you lingered, watching the dance of hands and flames, the tacos kept coming as if they knew you'd been waiting all week.

Somehow, the world shrank to that small, smoke-filled counter, where every taste, every sizzle, felt like home.

If you were so inclined, you could walk it all—roughly a four-mile round trip—but most of the time, we rode in the car, stopping only where we had to.

I'd press my nose to the window, eyes wide, trying to drink in the smells, the colors, the life of it all. Sometimes we stayed longer, visiting relatives, lingering over conversation and tortillas.

Other times, it was purely business: get what we needed, cross back over the border, return home. Either way, the city wrapped itself around us, stitching together family, culture, and the pulse of a childhood that felt infinite.

Sundays were for baseball.

I played in a Sunday league made up of the most mismatched collection of characters—young and old, has-beens and wanna-bes, all trying to prove something to someone. I used to cross the border on foot early Sunday mornings, the kind of early when even the churro carts were still asleep. I'd wave down a taxi outside the garitas and tell the driver to take me to La Jabonera—and he'd always give me that look, like I'd just requested a ride to 1953.

What most folks saw by then was a neighborhood stitched together from old foundations, stubborn families, and whatever the wind hadn't blown away.

But underneath it all were the ghostly remains of the Compañía Industrial Jabonera del Pacífico. Back in its prime, it handled enough cottonseed to perfume the whole valley in that unmistakable "aceites y esperanza" smell.

Cotton went out of style—polyester showed up like the new kid at school—and the once-mighty complex crumbled. The factories were abandoned, vandalized, and pulled apart brick by brick, leaving only memories, a few creaky homes, and a name that refused to die.

That's where El Primo lived—our unofficial uncle, official storyteller, and part-time philosopher of Sunday league baseball.

I'd find him outside his house, already stretching like he was about to be scouted by the Dodgers, wearing baseball pants so old they probably remembered the cotton boom themselves. His pride and joy, a sunburned Econoline van, sat parked at a heroic angle, squeaking and rattling like a lifelong smoker clearing its lungs, sending tiny shivers through the floor.

Climbing into that van felt like joining a pilgrimage: a ragtag procession rolling out of La Jabonera, past the ghosts of ginning plants, stray dogs, and early risers, heading toward dusty fields where legends were—and mostly weren't—made.

Looking back, it wasn't just a ride to a ball game. It was crossing through time, humor, and history, all in that rattling van with El Primo shouting, "¡Súbanse, que ya vamos tarde!"

The fields themselves were makeshift diamonds carved out of ranch land on the eastern outskirts of the city—pure grit and dust; nothing like the manicured fields across the border. Infields of deep, loose sand swallowed grounders whole, sending tiny clouds of grit into cleats and socks.

Outfields where irrigation canals doubled as warning tracks, and railroad tracks cut through the back corner like an extra foul line only the veterans understood. The sun baked every patch of dirt, carrying the faint smell of sweat and iron.

You didn't slide out there unless you were willing to sacrifice half your skin. You didn't complain, either. That was just baseball in Mexicali—raw, improvised, beautiful in its own crooked way.

Our equipment wasn't much better. Younger guys had decent-looking gear, slightly worn. The older guys carried gloves patched with mismatched leather, spikes ground down to nubs, held together with duct tape.

One guy used leather work gloves as batting gloves. And then there was the smell of Iodex—like Ben-Gay—slathered on arms and legs as if it were sunscreen. But these older guys could ball. They possessed a knowledge of the game unmatched, a wealth of experience.

Primo called *colmio.*

Games were intense. Everyone played like they were being scouted. Cars and trucks lined the sides of the fields; spectators were family, die-hard baseball aficionados, and anyone with nothing better to do. And in the midst of it all, you felt the pulse of the city—the old barrio, the van, the sand, the sun, and the laughter.

Baseball in Mexicali wasn't polished, it wasn't pretty, but it was ours.

I remember my first game like it was yesterday. Primo came up to me with an old Polaroid camera. "Ocupas una credencial," he said. He snapped my picture, then, with the help of another coach, cut it down and glued it to a scrap of old ID.

Using a rubber band and a marker, he drew the outline of a stamp over the photo and sealed it with clear tape.

"Toma, mijo," he said. "Cuando te pidan la credencial, enseña esto. Te llamas Juan José Cabrera." And just like that, I was a 27-year-old league member with 8 years of experience… despite being only fourteen.

I opened the game as lead-off, playing center field. I remember watching the opposing pitcher warm up—throwing serious heat. Primo came up, patted me on the butt, and said, "No, tiene nada. Es puro humo."

Then he sent me to the plate. The pitcher smiled, hurled a fastball meant to back me off, and I ended up on my butt. Somewhere behind the mound, I heard, "Dale otra… tiene miedo."

I shook it off.

Next pitch—PING!

The ball screamed off my bat, a sharp metallic crack that made my teeth tingle, soaring straight toward left-center. I pumped my knees high to avoid sinking into the loose dirt.

TRIPLE.

On my first at-bat. Two batters later, I scored on a single, high-fiving everyone in sight.

Later, in the dugout, one of the older players came up behind me. "Toma, mijo. Para celebrar." He handed me an ice-cold can of Tecate.

Drinking beer at games wasn't unusual—sometimes as early as nine in the morning. I gave him a look that screamed, *A beer? Now? Seriously?* He tapped me on the shoulder again. "Ándale, tómala, no pasa nada," and cracked it open.

I took a cautious sip, made a face, and set the can under the bench. This wasn't baseball back home. It was messy, rowdy, and perfectly Mexicali—the kind of baseball that left dust in your cleats, sunburn on your neck, and memories that lasted forever.

After games, we'd make it back to Primo's house, and depending on how the day went, we'd either celebrate or pretend it never happened. Not to brag, but we mostly celebrated—told the tales of the day's highlights. T

here was always good food—home-cooked, messy, comforting—and cold drinks that hit just right after running around all day. I'd grab a burrito, a soda, pack up my things, and catch a taxi back to the border, heading home with the flavors of the day still clinging to my fingers and the smell of frying tortillas tucked under my nose.

Summer brought a whole different level to trips across the border. The adults did what they did.

The kids? We got off to the inevitable mischief that unaccompanied minors in Mexicali inevitably found. A literal world waited to be conquered.

A trip to the local park could easily turn into a full-on soccer match—enough kids around to make it worthwhile, our shouts and laughter bouncing off walls, trees, and the sun-baked ground.

Later, we'd duck into the local arcade for cold drinks and a quick game. You'd place a coin on the bottom lip of the screen to mark your turn, the chirps and beeps of *Donkey Kong* echoing across the room.

In the next room, ping-pong balls rattled off paddles, sneakers squeaked against the worn floor, and the air buzzed with the perfect soundtrack to summer chaos—sticky fingers and all.

Other times, we stayed in the yard, playing with tops or marbles, stopping only to complete whatever chores Nana demanded.

And then there was the pure excitement of raspados down the block. Usually an old man with a cart, massive tin tubs hiding enormous blocks of ice under heavy woven sacks.

He'd run a metal planer over the ice, the shavings falling into a cup, then top it with one of a rainbow of homemade syrups—fresa, tamarindo, limón, ciruela, piña, sandía… mmmm. Gluttonous, icy, sugary goodness.

Trips to the movies were always an adventure. An aunt lived in the apartment above the theater, and she'd tell us exactly when to go.

My uncle would pack us all into the back of his old combi—a beat-up Volkswagen bus with no seats, no carpeting, nothing to hold on to except the backs of the driver and front passenger seats. "Riding in style," I'd say, gripping the sides and bouncing with every turn, trying not to spill the snacks we'd smuggled on board.

We'd knock at the back door, and she'd quietly open it, whispering that a movie was already playing. We were behind the screen.

A spiral staircase led up to her apartment—a treacherous climb in the dark, sending knees and elbows into unsuspecting railings, perfect for a clumsy summer memory.

Movie time meant the careful climb down to the theater and a quick stop at the snack counter: popcorn, jalapeño-spiked hotdogs, and fizzy sodas that left your fingers sticky.

Then it was off to the front-row seats, the smell of buttered popcorn blending with the faint mustiness of the old theater, the screen flickering to life and pulling us into another world.

I remember seeing *E.T.* when it first came out—an experience like no other—seated just behind the big screen, as if we had our own private showing, completely swallowed by the story and the magic of the lights.

Some Saturdays, Tata would pile us into the car and we'd male the trek over to the Arena Coliseo Mexicali for a little trouble and a lot of spectacle. One trip sticks in my mind more than most: the midget lucha libre.

A dozen diminutive acrobats, masks gleaming under the harsh arena lights, flipping, diving, and bouncing around the ring like it was made of trampolines.

Tata would chuckle, shaking his head, muttering, "Miren nomás… puro talento chiquito, pero con ganas grandotas." And he was right.

These tiny wrestlers—some barely taller than a grocery bag—launched themselves off ropes, tumbled across the mat, and slammed each other down with all the drama of full-sized heroes. The crowd went wild, roaring for every backflip, every near-fall, every exaggerated pin.

From our seats, we laughed, cheered, and sometimes ducked—Tata elbowing me in the ribs when a particularly ambitious luchador launched toward the edge of the ring. It was chaotic, loud, absurd, and absolutely brilliant. Somehow, in that tiny ring, a dozen little bodies could hold an entire arena captive.

And as always, crossing back over the border later that night, our ears still ringing with the roar of the crowd, I understood: Calexico and Mexicali might be separated by a line on a map, but those afternoons? They were pure, uncontainable magic.

Back in Calexico, life settled into something close to normal—at least as normal as a kid could hope for. It was a sharp contrast to the loose rules, spontaneous adventures, and controlled chaos of Mexicali, where every corner held a new surprise and every day felt a little wilder than the last.

School was school, chores were chores, and whenever we found even the smallest gap in the daily grind, mischief somehow slipped right in. There was always something to do—homework if we had it, tinkering with Dad if we were lucky, banana ball with my brother when we needed to burn off energy.

TV filled the quiet moments, too.

And later, when technology finally caught up to our little house, Atari and eventually Nintendo made their grand entrance, glowing like treasures in the living room. My mom had strict control over those machines; the moment she got tired of the beeps, explosions, and 8-bit chaos, off they went and we were tossed outside like yesterday's trash.

Some afternoons, we'd retreat to our rooms with a blank cassette in hand and a plan: capture the perfect song, right from the radio.

Making a mix tape was an art form, a careful science of timing, patience, and sheer luck. You'd sit there, pencil in hand, finger hovering over the record button, ears straining through the static as the DJ babbled endlessly, waiting for your song to come on.

When it was time to record, every second stretched out like taffy. You counted the beats, tapped the pencil on your knee, whispered the lyrics under your breath, willing the DJ to shut up, the ads to vanish, and the universe to pause until *your* moment came.

Timing was everything. Too early, and you captured the tail-end of the last song or an obnoxious DJ voice. Too late, and your favorite riff vanished into thin air, leaving a half-recorded mess of static and disappointment. There were expletives—quiet, muttered, and desperate—and fist pumps when it worked.

And when it finally did? Pure magic. You'd press play and listen, over and over, smiling like you'd stolen something from the heavens. That little cassette was more than music—it was a map of your life, your moods, your laughter, your crushes, your arguments with your siblings over who got the last side. It was fleeting, precious, and completely yours.

Making mix tapes taught patience. It taught strategy. It taught that sometimes the perfect thing doesn't happen the first time—but when it finally does, it's worth every second of waiting.

By the time the last song had faded and the tape clicked off, the day had already slipped a little further toward evening. The sun hung low in the sky, and boredom—or curiosity—began to nibble at the edges of our afternoons.

That's when we'd end up at my sister's video store, half to browse, half to stir up trouble, and fully to extend the magic of those long, soundtrack-filled afternoons.

My sister Norma worked at a place called Online Video, and whenever we were bored, we'd end up pestering her at work.

Most nights the place was slow, so we'd walk the eight or nine blocks down Heber Ave. to the store. Sometimes we arrived like civilized humans, slipping in quietly, pretending we were just there to "browse."

Other times… yeah, not so quiet. We came in like a pack of wild monkeys, making enough noise to wake the dead and definitely annoy my sister.

One time I got a little too caught up in the moment.

I barged in, basically kicked the door down, and announced my presence with a burp so loud and so deep it practically had subwoofers. In the perfect acoustics of that little video store, it echoed off every wall and rattled the VHS shelves like a small local earthquake.

Everyone froze—including the handful of customers who definitely hadn't signed up for this kind of entertainment. The second I realized we weren't alone, I felt my face go hot. I made the shameful walk around the counter… and right back out the door. Red as hell. My sister didn't even have to say a word.

I came back a little while later, but this time I made sure to peek through the window first, just in case there were any unsuspecting customers inside. When the coast was clear, I slipped in quietly. My sister just looked at me, shaking her head and laughing.

"Pendejo, What the hell was that?" she said, still trying to catch her breath.

I didn't have an answer—I just laughed too. What can you say after detonating an atomic burp-bomb in a video store?

Hanging out there was cool, though. There was always some movie playing on the little TV in the back, usually something she'd already seen a hundred times.

We'd help rewind the VHS tapes and put them back on the shelves, pretending we were employees even though we never actually did the job right.

In return, we got free rentals and sometimes snacks—chocolates, Red Vines, popcorn—the good stuff that always tasted better when you didn't have to pay for it.

When the store finally closed, we'd all head home, snack on leftovers, and maybe stay up late. Maybe. Tomorrow would come soon, and there'd be a whole new day to make memories.

In Calexico, the rhythm was slower, quieter—but no less full of life.

Kids on the street played stickball or tag until the sun began to dip behind the low desert hills. The corner store smelled of fresh tortillas, candy, and gasoline from the old trucks that rumbled by.

Neighbors waved from porches, and the hum of air conditioners mixed with the faint twang of a distant guitar. There was still mischief, but it moved differently here—a gentle push on a swing, a racing bike down the sidewalk, a borrowed ball tossed over a chain-link fence.

Even the simplest things had two flavors. Crossing the border might give you spicy tacos or sweet raspados, but here it was the little touches: the creak of a gate, the smell of roses in a front yard, your mom calling you for dinner.

Life was familiar, predictable—but never boring.

And somehow, that made it perfect.

Living in *Calexicali* meant learning to read both worlds.

One day you were shouting, dodging, laughing, and sweating in Mexicali; the next, you were riding your bike on a quiet Calexico street, watching the clouds turn pink, chewing on a peanut butter sandwich, and feeling at home in a different kind of chaos.

You learned to speak in two languages, to see two perspectives, to celebrate two kinds of joy—and somehow, it all blended into something only you could call yours.

It was messy.

It was confusing.

It was hilarious.

But it was home.

Two lunchboxes.

Two cities.

One kid.

Endless stories.

THE
GAMES
WE PLAYED

The Games We Played

We all grow up playing games. (Some of us still play games as adults; the games have just evolved).

Some are simple acts of imagination, little experiments in creativity. Others are just for fun—or to pass the time. Board games strewn across the kitchen table, cards clutched in sweaty hands, races through the yard for no reason other than the sheer joy of running (adult me still cringes and asks: why???).

It's all part of growing up, a patchwork of moments that teaches us, challenges us, and—most importantly—makes us laugh.

Growing up in a small town—and a small border town at that—these games weren't just pastimes; they were part of everyday life. Limits became opportunities, disadvantages turned into advantages.

Streets too narrow for bikes became obstacle courses.

Empty lots became stadiums.

The heat, the dust, the barking dogs—all of it was just part of the rules we made up as we went along.

It was common for us to make up games, and change the rules as we went along. Each game was a small adventure, a chaotic lesson in creativity, strategy, and the occasional disaster.

It was life, happening in real time.

No social media.

No likes.

No evidence of our questionable decision-making—thank God.

Just kids making the most of what they had, inventing worlds out of dirt lots, bottle caps, marbles, and whatever else we could get our hands on.

Back then, it really was that simple.

Marbles

When we weren't chasing each other around the yard, we were waging wars of a different kind—on the dirt patch under the mulberry trees.

Marbles were the go-to game for kids on both sides of the border; they were currency, status, and entertainment all rolled into one. It was especially a favorite among the boys at school (and a few fearless girls who could hold their own).

Kids walked around with pockets full of marbles clanking like loose change, much to the eternal irritation of teachers. Those same pockets were responsible for countless "tense negotiations" on the playground—exchanges so heated that I'm sure the principal questioned his career choices every time he had to act as arbitrator.

That dusty patch was our version of the stock exchange—a tiny arena where fortunes could be won or lost with a single flick of the thumb. Marbles changed hands like money at the market. Fortunes were made and lost—sometimes multiple times in a single afternoon.

Marbles came in every size, color, and material—each with its own value, each one coveted like treasure. Every marble had a role: some were strikers, some were pawns, and some were just plain elegant. And every kid had their favorites—the untouchables.

There were Cat's Eyes with their tiny flames of color, clearies that looked like frozen bubbles, and soft, opaque milkies that seemed poured from clouds.

Swirls spun ribbons of color like miniature galaxies, and aggies—earth-toned and heavy—always felt a little ancient.

Oversized shooters (bombones), especially the dense black ones streaked with red, could change the tide of a game (some kids carried them purely for intimidation) or pearls that shimmered like moonlit glass.

But the most coveted of all were the onyx-black beauties with hints of purple or green and, of course, the legendary steelies—cold, heavy, and capable of clearing a ring with a single perfect strike.

I had a handful of mine: two deep-black, heavy marbles that, if you held them up to the light just right, glowed faintly purple. A couple of larger strikers too, black with red lightning bolts trapped inside. And then the kingpin of them all—my stainless-steel striker.

It wasn't unusual for kids to meet up and make trades—quiet negotiations in the shade of a monkey bar, little generals preparing for war. It was all part of the strategy, almost like chess… just without the board.

During recess we crouched low, pockets full of tiny spheres, eyes narrowed in concentration.

Some kids played ollitos, shooting marbles into tiny holes. The object of the game? Honestly, I can't quite remember—but there was always a winner, and inevitably, a loser.

Oh wait, I think I remember now. Four holes: two at the top, one in the center, one at the end. You'd flick your marble toward the top holes. Make it? You got to shoot at the next two holes, back and forth, to claim victory.

Miss it? Your opponent got a chance to knock you out.

And then there was the cheat code: the copis.

What's that?

Basically, a tiny mound of dirt you made with your dusty paw to lift an opponent's marble ever so slightly, giving yourself a better shot. It required skill—or luck, or a combination of both.

I remember crouching in the dirt, palm curled, thumb cocked, staring down a marble like it was the final boss. "You're going down, Supernova," I whispered, my heart pounding. A flick, a clink, a wobble—and sometimes… glory. Other times… ashes.

One-on-one.

You vs. me.

For keeps.

Losers handed over their marbles.

And somehow… the game always ended. Eventually. Nobody quite knew how, but the stakes?

Oh, they felt very real.

Others played for keeps in the ring.

One kid would grab the nearest stick and scrape out a "circle" in the dirt—though more often than not it looked like a lopsided potato or a misshapen tortilla. Didn't matter. That was the arena.

To enter, you only had to toss ten marbles into the ring.

The rules were simple: knock marbles out, and whatever rolled free of the ring was yours. Miss? and your prized shooter might stay stranded in the circle—suddenly fair game for the next kid with a steadier hand and nerves of steel.

If you were good, it was the fastest way to build a small fortune in marbles. The game always drew a crowd, kids gathering around like spectators at a backyard cockfight. I swear there were even side bets being made—nothing but marbles, of course, but still. Probably the earliest taste of gambling any of us ever got.

I remember once walking into school with three marbles in my pocket and heading home with two pockets full. Another time, I lost them all—and blamed my brother for the bad luck.

More often than not, I was on the winning side of things. I considered myself a pretty good Marble player. A champion, if you will. I was known for hustling kids out of their marble holdings.

At home, I had a method to the madness that was marble storage. I had two massive five-gallon jugs where I kept all the "lower-class" marbles—the ones most often offered up as tribute. The ones you didn't mind losing: clearies, cat's eyes, and milkies. cheap, but plentiful. I kept these jugs out back, next to my dad's tool shed. My mom would often grab handfuls to use as table decorations, adding a little flair to her floral arrangements.

Most of the bombones and strikers lived in a box next to my bed. Always within eyesight, always under strict inventory—I knew exactly what I had at all times.

And then, of course, there were my black onyx and steelies, my *preferiti.* These were hidden away from prying eyes, in a secret spot only I knew about (though my brother was always scheming to find them). They came out only when a conquest demanded a statement.

Marbles weren't just toys—they were tiny universes, each flick a battle in our miniature galaxy.

And we?

We were fearless warriors, strategists, and, every now and then, criminals of the sandbox stock market.

Bottle Rocket Wars

Other times, we sought higher stakes—rockets in hand and the barrio in Mexicali as our battlefield. Now that I think about it, it's a wonder we even had brains. It was cowboys and Indians, but with airborne flaming projectiles—basically mini flying bombs.

And where else could a teenager get live fireworks and shoot them at each other without an adult batting an eye? Across the border, of course—in Mexicali, the land of limitless possibilities.

In those days, fireworks were basically a year-round sport in Mexicali. You didn't need a holiday—just a free afternoon, a handful of pesos, and the kind of questionable judgment only a border-town childhood could nurture.

Our war games weren't fought in neat backyards or manicured cul-de-sacs. No—our battlefield was everywhere: empty lots between houses, dusty gaps where construction had stalled for years, or wide-open stretches of scrub on the outskirts of the barrio. Anywhere with dirt, space, and no adults. That was sacred ground. It was sovereign territory.

We'd scrounge together whatever change we could find—pesos from couch cushions, coins from car ashtrays, crumpled bills saved from errands—and make the pilgrimage to the nearest mercado. The old man behind the counter never asked questions. He just nodded, shoved a mixed crate of bottle rockets across the counter, and watched us leave like a priest handing over holy relics.

The crate was our artillery, our treasure chest—our weekend distilled into cardboard and paper fuses.

The rules of engagement were simple:

No parents.
No squealing.
No snitching.
No crying loud enough for an adult to hear.

And no aiming at heads or faces (this rule was regularly and willfully broken relentlessly). It was one of those "official guidelines" everyone pretended to respect until the moment things got interesting—kind of like the posted speed limit on Highway 111.

Teams were selected, and the battles began. Each 'soldier' picked a bottle from which to launch. The green 7-Up bottle seemed to be the sturdiest—its glass thick, almost smug, as if it knew it would survive the chaos. Alfonso grabbed one with a grin, gave it a careful inspect, and muttered, "This one's mine. She won't betray me."

Jorge snorted. "All bottles betray eventually. Don't get attached."

Fuses were lit, and hisses erupted as rockets trembled with potential energy. The smell of sulfur drifted through the lot, mingling with dust and sun-baked weeds, and every launch carried the promise of glory—or a minor singe. We crouched behind crates and bushes, counting down together:

"Three… two… one… GO!"

The first rockets shot into the sky, some arcing beautifully, others zigzagging like drunk birds. One narrowly missed Alfonso's head, leaving him ducking and swearing under his breath, while the green 7-Up bottle survived its debut unscathed, earning a sort of silent respect from everyone on the battlefield.

Bottle rockets hissed and fumed, flipping, spinning, and occasionally exploding on impact, turning cars, dirt mounds, and makeshift forts into temporary casualties of war.

Each launch sent us ducking, shrieking, and laughing all at once, the air thick with sulfur smoke, dust, and the reckless exhilaration that only a border-town childhood could produce.

Injuries were common, expected, and never documented. Battlefield medicine was the only acceptable form:

Scraped knee? Rub dirt on it.
Burnt thumb? Blow on it until the sting dulled.
Small cut from a misfire? Wrap it in your shirt and keep firing.

Because telling your parents meant the crate vanished, lectures began, and the fun—our sacred war—ended.

Reinforcement munitions waited in the dirt like tiny missiles, trembling with potential energy. Alfonso crouched low, eyes glittering with mischief.

"Ready… set… GO!" he shouted, and the battlefield erupted.

We darted between cactus and chain-link fences, leaping over crates and dodging the occasional tumbleweed. Junked cars became fortresses.

Overturned boxes were barricades. Once we found cover, we'd load a bottle, light the fuse, and take aim. Each rocket hissed like a miniature dragon, leaving behind a streak of sulfur-smelling smoke.

"Watch out!" I yelled, ducking as one zipped past my ear and smacked Jorge square in the shoulder.

We screamed, scrambled, slipped across dust and gravel, laughing until our sides hurt. Every so often someone paused to reload, crouched behind a bush or mailbox, peeking out like tiny soldiers plotting the next attack.

The air thickened with smoke. Spent fuses littered the ground. Mud from leftover puddles created a new hazard—sliding, flailing, and accidental face-plants became part of the strategy.

By sundown, the lot was shrouded in smoke, cardboard scorched, the air thick with gunpowder and triumph. We were sweaty, filthy, victorious—and ready to reload and do it all again.

And then came the ultimate betrayal.

Someone's little sister, armed with a garden hose and a fierce sense of justice, stormed the battlefield.

"No more chaos today!" she declared, blasting Jorge with icy water and sending him sprawling.

The rockets sputtered. The battlefield sizzled. A wet sulfur-smelling fog settled over the lot.

For a moment, we stood there—dripping, smoky, defeated.

But we knew better.

Tomorrow, the battlefield would be ready again. Rockets reloaded. Dirt patched. Spirits revived. And the war—louder, messier, and infinitely more chaotic—would resume.

Unless something else came up.

And it often did.

The Mud Bowl

Before video games, before cell phones, before anyone cared about ACLs or insurance deductibles, there was only one sport that truly tested the heart of a border-town kid: mud football. Not regular football—no, that was for dry days and responsible children.

I'm talking about the post-storm, ankle-deep, shoe-eating, friendship-testing battlefield of pure chaos we affectionately called *The Mud Bowl*. The storm clouds were barely gone before we were already lacing up our ruined sneakers and charging the fields like we had something to prove.

This wasn't a regular thing. Sure, Calexico saw rain from time to time, but never the kind that made anything *worthwhile*. Most storms were just light sprinkles that evaporated before they even hit the sidewalk. But every now and then—maybe once or twice a year if the weather gods were bored—we'd get one of those world-altering downpours.

World-altering *to us*, anyway.

Those were the days the gutters overflowed, the streets turned to chocolate milk, and every kid in the neighborhood felt something stirring deep inside—a primal call, a muddy destiny.

Those rare storms separated the kids from the boys… or something like that. Because when the rain stopped and the puddles settled, there was only one logical thing left to do:

Declare The Mud Bowl officially underway.

There were enough of us in the neighborhood to throw down the best game of mud football anywhere. Most of the time, the street was our field—sidewalks as sidelines, parked cars as the only obstacles, and the occasional honking car reminding us we weren't in the NFL.

The field was unrecognizable after the rain, a squishy, brown wasteland littered with puddles deep enough to swallow a sneaker. The ball itself was slick and uncooperative, coated in mud so thick it left streaks on anyone who dared touch it.

"Pass it! Pass it!" shouted David, arms flailing, legs slipping with every step.

"I'm trying!" Bobby yelled, face caked in mud, goggles of brown smeared over his eyes. He dove for the ball and came up with a handful of nothing but muck, sliding on his stomach like a toddler on a slip-and-slide.

Danny charged forward, ball in hand, slipping three times before he managed to stagger ten feet. "Don't… stop… me!" he gasped, arms pumping, before planting a foot in a puddle and going down in a spectacular, slow-motion belly flop. Mud geysered upward, hitting anyone standing within a five-foot radius.

Somewhere nearby, Javier attempted a dramatic interception, leaping into the air like he'd seen in the pros. He landed flat on his back with a squelch, the ball bouncing off his chest and rolling straight into Douglas' path. "I'm invincible!" Douglas shouted, moments before slipping and sliding into Jorge, who yelped as if a small mud monster had attacked him.

The sidelines were no less chaotic. Half the team was trying to sprint, half was trying not to get stuck in a mud pit that had become a legitimate hazard. "Watch the puddle!" someone shouted… seconds too late. By now, everyone was coated head to toe in brown, shoes gone or full of sludge, jerseys caked in mud, hair plastered to their faces.

Even the "referee," Tommy, had given up. He sat on a bench, wiping mud off his clipboard with one hand while eating chips with the other, muttering, "This isn't football. This is war… with mud."

And then… the legendary plays began.

Bobby dove for the ball in slow motion. Mud exploded around him like fireworks. His arms flailed, one leg kicked skyward, and for a brief moment, time itself seemed to pause as he twisted mid-air and missed the ball by a mere inch.

Miguel ran full tilt, the ball tucked under his arm, eyes wide. His foot caught a hidden puddle, and—pause—the world slowed. His arms windmilled, his hair plastered to his mud-smeared face, and he slid across the field like a cartoon superhero crashing through a chocolate river.

Jorge attempted a tackle, leaping like a professional linebacker—but the mud betrayed him. Slow-motion glory: he spun, flailed, and landed face-first, sending a geyser of mud skyward in perfect, cinematic arcs. It rained down on spectators, who ducked and screamed in exaggerated horror.

Javier, not to be outdone, launched himself at the ball with a dramatic jump worthy of a sports movie trailer. His shoes left the ground, mud dripping in heroic streams, arms outstretched like wings. And then—splat—he hit the puddle, sending a tsunami of brown water toward the goal line.

The ball, however, bounced… and bounced… and bounced… straight into David's waiting hands, somehow avoiding disaster.

Every tackle, slip, and slide was amplified in glorious, ridiculous slow motion: hair flying, mud arcing through the air like liquid confetti, shouts and laughter echoing across the battlefield. Even the defeated players looked like heroes in a highlight reel, limbs flailing with exaggerated style, triumph and chaos perfectly intertwined.

No one kept score. No one cared. Shoes were gone, jerseys shredded, and every player coated from head to toe in mud—but every single one of us had a slow-motion moment of absolute glory. The field was a disaster, yes—but it was *our* disaster, and somehow, that made us champions.

By the end, we were caked in brown, shoes gone, jerseys forgotten—just a band of muddy gladiators, undefeated in the history of backyard sports.

Getting home, though? That was a whole other adventure—or should I say, *Judgment Day.*

Mom must have had some sort of radar, because no matter what she was doing, she somehow sensed us coming and intercepted us before we even reached the porch.

There she would be, hose in hand, eyes narrowing like a drill sergeant. "Off with the mud!" she barked, and off we went, a chorus of groans, shrieks, and water splashing everywhere. Every inch of skin, every strand of hair, every last fleck of mud had to be blasted away.

But that wasn't enough. Oh no. The final ritual: the *air-dry.*

We had to stand there, dripping and shivering, until the mud-free verdict was officially granted. Only then could we cross the threshold, soggy but victorious, into the house—battered, bruised, but undefeated in spirit.

Looking back, it wasn't really about winning or losing. It was about the smell of dust in the air, the sting of mud on scraped knees, the thrill of launching a bottle rocket, or flicking a marble with just the right touch.

It was about the sound of laughter echoing across streets too narrow for normal games, and the fierce, ridiculous joy of claiming a tiny patch of the world as our own.

These games—chaotic, messy, fearless—were lessons in creativity, courage, and camaraderie. They taught us how to take risks, how to fail spectacularly, and how to get back up, laughing, ready for the next round.

Hot Wheels Havoc

The carpet in the living room became a battlefield, a city, a stunt track all at once. My brother Javier and I crouched low, eyes gleaming with mischief, Hot Wheels clutched like tiny, precious war machines.

"Ready… set… blow it up!" he shouted, holding a makeshift launcher made from a cardboard ramp and a rubber band.

Inside, we built cities of blocks, highways of books, and bridges of rulers. Each car had a role: hero, villain, daredevil stunt racer. Sometimes, the buildings collapsed spectacularly on their own. Sometimes, they needed a little… encouragement.

Explosions were improvised: marbles toppled towers, coins ricocheted like shrapnel, pencil shavings puffed up as smoke.

Before any chaos, though, there was the artistry. Javier and I, self-appointed resident Hot Wheels artists, gave each car its own personality. Flames on the hood, racing stripes, hand-painted sparkles—no car left the garage without its signature look.

Sometimes, the chaos got too much. A block tower collapsed on Mom's slipper. A racecar skidded under the couch. That's when she sighed and declared: "Outside! This is why we can't have nice things!"

And that's where the real fun began.

Out in the yard, Hot Wheels became missiles of mass destruction. Fireworks were involved—carefully, sort of. Cars strapped to bottle rockets, ramps became launch pads, every crash a glorious, noisy spectacle. “Boom!” A red car flipped spectacularly. “Direct hit!” I cheered as a blue one tumbled, leaving a trail of smoke and a faint sulfur smell.

The neighborhood dogs were not impressed. Barking erupted from every yard, teeth bared, tails high with suspicion. From across the street, Señora Morales shook her fist. “You’re scaring the dogs again!” My brother and I ducked behind a bush, snickering at the chaos we had unleashed.

And yet, as artists, we never left a car truly broken. After the smoke cleared, if a Hot Wheels survived, it was carefully rescued, scrubbed clean, and repainted. Dents became design features, scorch marks turned into racing stripes. Every car had its second life, ready to wreak havoc—or look fabulous—again.

By the end, the driveway looked like a miniature war zone. Cars flipped, ramps broken, fireworks spent. And we? Sticky with glue, smudged with soot, hair plastered to our foreheads, laughing until our sides hurt. Sometimes creation happens inside. Sometimes chaos forces us outside.

And sometimes, the only way to win is to watch a Hot Wheels car fly through the air, explode in glorious fashion, and then bring it home, scrub it clean, and make it shine again—because that’s when the fun is real.

KISS Dolls Gone Wild

If Hot Wheels taught us how to cause chaos, my sister’s dolls taught us how to turn artistry into controlled disaster. Javier and I, ever the resident artists, had a knack for taking ordinary objects and giving them personality—whether it was a streak of racing stripes on a car or a face-painted doll ready to rock.

Boredom struck one afternoon, and suddenly, those pristine dolls lined up on her shelf were not just toys—they were a rock band waiting to perform. And so began our next masterpiece of mischief: KISS.

Armed with markers, paint, and the reckless creativity only boredom can summon, we transformed the dolls into rock stars. Black-and-white face paint, glittery costumes, miniature guitars drawn on tiny hands.

Each doll had a personality, a flair, a tiny stage-ready attitude.

"Welcome to the hottest concert in the living room!" Javier announced, gesturing dramatically.

We set the dolls on a floor stage built from books and shoeboxes. They stood tall—or as tall as dolls can—ready to rock out. And for a moment, the living room became Madison Square Garden.

I air-guitared like a man possessed, Javier headbanged with full commitment, and the dolls—silent but fierce—performed their tiny hits.

Then, somehow, the concert got out of hand. One of us, trying to make it "real," struck a small match for dramatic stage effects. I don't recall where the idea to use a can of Aquanet to mimic pyrotechnics came from, but at the time, it seemed brilliant. Or so we thought.

One tiny flame, a faint sizzle, a burst of Aquanet—and suddenly, a doll's glittery costume caught fire.

Panicked, we scrambled to save them, but it was too late. The drummer doll's hair curled, the guitarist melted into an unrecognizable lump, and the stage—a precarious pile of books—was slightly scorched.

We stood there, jaws dropped, as our masterpiece of rock and rebellion became a smoky, melted disaster.

And somewhere in the background, I'm pretty sure my sister screamed.

Loudly.

Very loudly.

"Worth it," Javier whispered, holding up a partially melted doll like a victory trophy.

Because in our world, boredom plus creativity always equals chaos—and sometimes, that chaos burns, *literally*.

***

Growing up in a small border town, we didn't just play games; we built memories that stuck like mud in our hair, shaping a childhood that—even now—feels impossibly alive.

We never needed rules carved in stone, referees with whistles, or neatly lined fields. We made do with what we had: cracked sidewalks, dusty alleys, busted bikes, mismatched marbles, muddy cul-de-sacs, and imaginations big enough to transform all of it into something epic.

Sure, there were plenty of other games—the typical stuff: baseball, riding our bikes, even jumping La Rampa when we felt brave—or reckless—enough.

Video games were still new, and most of us didn't have them anyway. Card games, board games, darts…the list goes on.

But few—very few—matched the creativity, the chaos, and the sheer bravado of the games we invented. The kind that pushed imagination to its limits and pushed *us* right to the brink of self-demise, grinning the whole way.

We didn't realize it then, but every game we played stitched another color into the quilt of our childhood. The heat, the dust, the border-town quirks, the chaos we invented, the rules we made up and broke, the worlds we built out of cardboard, dirt, and pure imagination—those were the things that shaped us long before we knew what shaping even meant.

Maybe that's why those memories feel larger than life now. The fields might've been small, the equipment improvised, the players barely coordinated—but the joy? The adventure? The sense that *anything* could happen on a random Tuesday afternoon?

That was enormous.

We weren't just killing time.

We were living it.

Middle School Madness

Middle School Madness

Middle school has got to be the most confusing time in a child's journey to adulthood.

It's like the universe hands every eleven-year-old a "starter pack" for growing up—half training wheels, half emotional roller coaster—and then walks away whistling, hoping for the best.

This is the era when you get your first taste of freedom, which usually means being trusted to walk to class alone and not immediately joining a roaming pack of gremlins jumping on trash cans.

It's when attitudes start to change, and a kid's voice can shift from "Sure, Mom" to "You don't understand my life" in under four seconds.

Friendships evolve daily, sometimes hourly. One minute you're inseparable because you both like the same pencil sharpener; the next, you're enemies because someone stole your seat at lunch.

And then—there it is—you start noticing the opposite sex in a "different" way. A deeply confusing, heart-thumping, sweat-triggering way that makes absolutely no sense. One day you're trading Pokémon cards; the next you're writing someone's name on your binder and pretending you didn't.

But the wildest part?

A middle schooler can go from child to adult to toddler in under 30 seconds. It's breathtaking. Olympic-level mood swings. Sometimes I wonder if NASA should study us instead of rockets.

Picture it:
A kid is discussing their future plans with the seriousness of a tax accountant— "I'm going to be an engineer or maybe an astronaut, but I'm still weighing the pros and cons."

Ten seconds later, that same kid is sprinting down the hallway making lightsaber noises while eating a fruit roll-up like it's a competitive sport.

Twenty seconds later, they're crying because someone looked at them "weird."

By the thirty-second mark they're laughing hysterically because their friend burped.

Middle school is basically a live-action telenovela acted out by people who still don't know how to properly apply deodorant.

It's confusing.

It's chaotic.

It's occasionally smelly.

But it's also magic—the messy, awkward bridge between who you were and who you're trying so hard to become.

As a middle school teacher (and eventually a school principal), I had a first-row seat to the daily, magical madness that is middle school in Calexico.

Think of it as educational Disneyland—if Disneyland had mood swings, bilingual announcements, and a student body that could go from angelic to "what just happened?" before the bell finished ringing.

Middle school is already entertaining everywhere, but in a border town?

It's a whole different sport.

Everything happens in two languages, two cultures, and somehow all of it translates into the common visual language and cultural shorthand that only those of us from "Calexicali" can fully comprehend.

You haven't lived until you've watched a kid get scolded in English, respond in Spanish, and then switch to Spanglish mid-excuse, leaving the teacher looking like she just read a foreign film script. It's like watching a linguistic triathlon.

Even the drama comes in two versions—one for each audience.

A playground argument might start in English, escalate in Spanish, and reach its grand finale in silent eyebrow gestures that communicate more than any sentence ever could.

And the fashion choices—*ay Dios mío.*

One kid shows up dressed like he's applying for a mortgage; the next looks like he rolled out of bed and lost the fight with the bedsheet. And then there's always that group walking around like a telenovela just broke out in PE.

But the best part?

The way these kids move between worlds with absolute confidence. They can complain about homework in English, gossip in Spanish, and describe a TikTok in Spanglish so thick it deserves its own dialect.

They'll eat Hot Cheetos for breakfast and still ask if the cafeteria has salsa. They'll chant "Let's go, Bulldogs!" at the rally and "¡Arriba las Chivas!" five minutes later at lunch.

They're border kids—smart, scrappy, funny, dramatic, bilingual, bicultural, and powered by Takis.

Times were vastly different in the early '80s when I went to middle school (De Anza Junior High School, if you must know—home of questionable fashion, legendary cafeteria burritos, and at least three unexplainable smells at any given moment).

Oh sure, kids from both sides of the border came to school back then too. And yes, the daily, non-academic happenings were just as bilingual—nay, bicultural—though none of us had the vocabulary at the time to describe it so academically. We just knew life was lived in English, Spanish, and whatever mixture your brain defaulted to when you were running late to class and trying not to get caught chewing gum.

We had the cholos, who traveled in slow-motion packs like a low-budget action movie. Their pants were crisp, hair nets perfectly taut, and their swagger suggested they'd survived at least one telenovela-level confrontation before lunch.

Then there were the O.P.s, named so because of their dedication—no, their spiritual alignment—with Ocean Pacific brand clothing. These kids looked like they were either on their way to the beach or accidentally time-traveled from a surfboard convention. Shorts neon, hair feathered, and walk screaming: "I either just rode a wave or got lost on the way to Mexico City."

And of course, there was everyone else.

The rest of us misfits, floaters, and regular kids who didn't fit neatly into any category. We were just trying to survive adolescence without tripping in front of our crush or accidentally joining the wrong friend group during lunch.

Some of us were still learning how to use deodorant correctly; others were navigating the treacherous journey from boys' size 12 to men's size confusion.

It was like a border-town, Mexican-American, middle school version of *The Outsiders*—only instead of "Stay gold, Ponyboy," it was more like, "Stay cool, vato… and don't let your mom catch you slicking your hair with her Alberto VO5."

Back then, middle school wasn't about belonging to a group.

It was about surviving the day—dodging drama, navigating the social caste system, and pretending you understood every single reference your older cousin made so you wouldn't look like a total niño.

Middle school in Calexico wasn't just school—it was basic training for life on the border. One minute you were conjugating English verbs, the next you were deciphering the unwritten laws of hallway etiquette.

You learned quickly that the fastest way to get roasted was to show up wearing something brand new. It didn't matter if your mom saved three paychecks for those shoes—you were going to hear about it from someone.

But for all its awkward chaos, those days were magic—loud, sweaty, bilingual magic. The kind that sticks with you long after you've grown up, become a teacher, and found yourself watching a new generation of kids replay the same middle school novela you once starred in.

Mischief in middle school has a unique flavor all its own.

Even now, middle school travesuras are both wildly creative and completely predictable—if you're paying attention. Middle schoolers are the biggest copycats on the planet.

Any and all trends, challenges, behaviors, sounds, dances, or bizarre rituals discovered on the internet are unapologetically copied and re-enacted ad nauseam.

It's absurdly simple—and yet, I think that's the genius of middle school life-lessons. These kids live in a perpetual loop of imitation, enthusiasm, and questionable decision-making. And honestly? It’s a beautiful mess.

Teachers on lunch duty know this better than anyone. You can spot a trend brewing from 200 yards away:

“You see that?”

“Yup.”

“You gonna tell him or should I?”

“Nah. Wait for it.”

The thing about middle school mischief is that it follows a script only the adults know by heart. First comes the idea—usually whispered, poorly disguised, and involving at least one kid saying, “Bro, trust me.”

Then comes the execution—sloppy, enthusiastic, and scientifically guaranteed to end in chaos. And finally, the fallout—the moment when they realize that maybe, just maybe, the plan wasn’t as foolproof as advertised.

We see it as the ideas take root in their immature minds, as the realization hits their eyes—like invisible signals that only we who have been there can see.

And the best part? It’s the SAME script we lived through in the ’80s at De Anza. Different decade, different slang, different shoes—but the travesuras? Identical.

Kids still try to sneak-run behind bushes.
Still attempt to launch themselves off benches.
Still hide from teachers who have been catching the same tricks for thirty years.

Middle schoolers honestly believe they invented mischief. Teachers know they’re watching the reboot.

For me, middle school was the beginning of my self-discovery journey—a place where I slowly realized who I was. And let me tell you, I didn't fit into any category. I was so awkward, I couldn't even fit in with the awkward kids.

Ain't that something?!

I was the poster boy for ADHD long before it was a thing—a whirlwind of energy packed into a 70-pound bundle of chaos. I doodled endlessly on everything. Every textbook was a battlefield of little drawings in the margins. By the time a teacher picked one up, it looked like a *Mad Magazine* special edition. Duplo copies of classwork? Half-finished and covered in doodles. Tests? Covered in doodles. Even the kid who sat in front of me in half my classes—the one who constantly fell asleep—somehow ended up with doodles on his arms. My desk? You better believe it: doodles. Everywhere.

During seventh grade, I learned calligraphy—and not in a "school supply catalog" way, but in a "your teacher is at the end of his rope and your principal just realized you might be a creative tornado" way.

It started with a frustrated teacher and a conference with my parents and the principal. One day, in the middle of a lecture, the teacher caught me drawing in my notebook. He snatched it and said he was calling my parents. Blah, blah, blah… like that would stop me.

A couple of days later, I found myself in the principal's office with Mr. Western, the assistant principal, Mr. James, my teacher, and my parents. Mr. Western looked at me like he was studying a rare species—the hyper-doodling middle schooler.

Mr. Western: "Mariano, why are you always drawing in your notebook… and on your tests? Do you draw on everything?"

Me: "Yup."

Mr. Western: “Why?”

Me: “It’s what I think of when the teacher is talking.”

Mr. Western: “So these drawings… are your class notes?”

Me: “Yup.”

Mr. Western: “You draw what comes to mind when your teacher is lecturing…?”

Me: “Yup.”

Mr. Western: “So… if I pick a page at random, you can tell me the topic of the day?”

Me: “Probably…”

He flipped to a random page, squinted at my doodles, and asked, “Tell me about this.” I squinted back, trying to translate a swirl of stick figures, swords, and a dinosaur wearing a crown. “Uhm… that was the day we started the Crusades.”

Mr. Western looked at the teacher. He nodded. “Yes, that is correct.”

He looked at my parents, closed the notebook, and handed it back. “Mr. and Mrs. Velez, you may go. Mariano, back to class. We’ll talk later.”

The next day, the teacher pulled me aside. “Finish the worksheet, then come over to this table and work on a special project.” He handed me calligraphy markers and a drawing pad. Just like that, I went from classroom menace to official teacher helper.

Weeks later, I was lettering projects for other teachers. My doodles had leveled up into actual calligraphy, and suddenly my notebook wasn’t just chaos—it was an educational art form.

Some months later, my calligraphy earned me the honor of making a nameplate for Mr. Western's office door. The same man who once questioned why I couldn't sit still now proudly displayed my work. Quiet victory. Funny reminder that middle school chaos sometimes grows into brilliance.

Calligraphy skills couldn't save me from Mrs. Tang and Home Ec.

Take caramel popcorn balls. Everyone else followed instructions. I had… creative ideas.

Making the popcorn? Easy. The caramel? Well…

I spread my popcorn across the desk, edge to edge, like a sticky, buttery carpet. Doubled the caramel recipe. Poured it all on top. Mixing bowl? Totally unnecessary. Who needed a bowl anyway?

Not me. It was just in the way.

Mrs. Tang made her rounds, nodding approvingly at everyone else. By the time she reached me, she did a slow, dramatic facepalm, muttered something in what sounded like Chinese, and it was clear—she was not happy.

She went to call the assistant principal. And in the precious minutes it took her to do that, the caramel set enough for me to peel it off the desk and roll it into a giant caramel popcorn stick—like a baseball bat forged from sugar, chaos, and middle school genius.

Enter Mr. James. One look at the popcorn stick, then at me. The infamous walk of doom began. Passing Mr. Western's office, he leaned out: "Calligraphy isn't gonna help you with this one."

Detention. The popcorn stick? Legendary office snack.

There was a series of other "minor" incidents throughout junior high. Not as legendary as the caramel popcorn stick, but certainly enough to keep me—and my comrades-in-arms—on Mr. James' radar.

The Belching Brigade: Six of us walked around belching. Timeless. Hilarious. Adults enraged. Explaining it to parents? Comedy gold.

The Lizard Heist: Same six-pack captured lizards, placed them in a paper bag… which somehow ended up in Mrs. George's desk. Lizards leapt like tiny missiles. She sprinted to the nurse. In-school suspension for us. Lesson learned? Sort of.

The Lunch Freedom Experiment: Open campus meant downtown Oasis Hotdogs adventures. Always late. Always detention.

Worth it. Every. Single. Time.

It was also around this time that we noticed the opposite sex in a "different" way.

Sometimes we got sent to the office on purpose—the clerk at the front was, shall we say, *shapely in all the right places*. We volunteered for anything involving the office: delivering attendance slips, picking up packages. Every trip became a field trip with perks.

The rest of middle school was a continuous series of little experiences—first taste of sports, campus travel, crushes, report cards, and the delicate art of forging signatures to hide F's in math.

PE's mile run loomed like punishment designed specifically for your middle school body. Excuses were invented daily: "I left my shoelaces at home… again." "Wait, do we have to run today?"

Middle school was a mix of small rebellions, minor victories, and personal experiments in surviving—sometimes thriving—amid chaos, hormones, and the mysterious gravitational pull of every crush in the building.

Looking back, it was a trial by fire, a rollercoaster of awkwardness, sticky desks, and questionable decisions that somehow forged the people we were becoming.

We learned that belching could be weaponized, caramel could be turned into a lethal weapon, and a well-timed doodle could earn you a place in school history—or at least detention.

We learned the delicate art of negotiating with authority, surviving the cafeteria, and decoding the complex social currency of hallways, buses, and shade structures.

Most importantly, we learned that being a little chaotic, a little awkward, and a little brave didn't just survive middle school—it thrived in it.

And somewhere in the mess, the laughter, the sugar-fueled escapades, and the endless Spanglish negotiations, we discovered that growing up wasn't about fitting in—it was about creating your own kind of legendary chaos, one sticky, glorious misstep at a time.

DAY
CAMP
DI@RIES

Day Camp Diaries

Before I figured out what I wanted to do with my life—or even what I was *supposed* to be doing as a student at Imperial Valley College—I found myself with a job that didn't feel like a job at all. If you'd asked me then, I probably would have said it was just play disguised as responsibility.

Most weekends and during the long breaks and summer, I traded textbooks for glue sticks, whistles, and a herd of sugar-fueled kids.

I showed up, put on a nametag, and somehow got paid to play games, referee chaos, and make sure tiny humans didn't destroy the universe… or at least the community center.

When you hear "summer camp," you might picture kids whisked away in vans, lugging haphazardly packed duffel bags, shipped off to some far-flung campground for a summer of "character building" and kumbaya bonding. Well… yeah—if you've watched enough movies, that's exactly what you've seen.

The reality?

Not all camps are like that. Some are closer to home, don't require bug spray rations, and the only wildlife you'll encounter is a rogue pigeon wandering into the gym.

Ours was a day camp—part school district, part Parks and Rec—all babysitting, all chaos, all fun.

It wasn't work in the traditional sense. There were no real rigid schedules, no endless paperwork, no soul-crushing monotony—just five days of controlled madness, laughter, and moments of pure, unfiltered fun. In hindsight, it was a preview of what my career would eventually become: guiding, encouraging, and laughing alongside people as they learned and grew.

Hosted at the local community center—the kind of place that effortlessly flips from quinceanera receptions to bingo nights to kids' camps without missing a beat. No cabins, no campfire songs, no counselors named "Moose."

Just five days of pure, unfiltered chaos—kids camp style.

Instead of sprawling campgrounds, we had a large indoor space—a "quinceañera hall" repurposed as an all-inclusive arena for the behavioral arts of summer.

Closest to the kitchen, tables were set up in a makeshift circle—perfect for budding artists to sling paint, mold clay, and generally make a mess before calling it art. In the far corner, tumbling mats sat beside miniature soccer goals for P.E.

Outside, the "multipurpose grass area"—really just the side garden with a few weeds—was prime turf for anything from relay races to impromptu mud negotiations.

Every morning, kids tumbled in like a small-scale stampede—some still sleepy, some bouncing like they'd already downed three Capri Suns.

We ran two shifts: mornings from 8:30 to 11:30, afternoons from 1 to 4. In between, I drank enough coffee to keep a small town awake and wondered how kids never run out of energy.

I always greeted the munchkins at the door, crouched like a catcher, handing out "low fives" as they bounced in. At just a smidge taller than a yardstick, most of these little changuitos could barely reach my hand, but they'd leap like it was the final jump in the Olympics.

Some were still rubbing sleep out of their eyes, others came in already vibrating with enough energy to power the ceiling fans.

Within minutes, they'd scatter—half to the art tables, half to the tumbling mats—and the quiet, orderly room I'd set up that morning transformed into a living, breathing piñata of noise and motion.

The activities were a curious mix of old-school classics and "wait, what even is that?"

Take crab ball, for instance—a wild twist on soccer where the players crab-walk around: hands and feet on the ground, backs arched like crustaceans trying out for the circus.

It's part athletic challenge, part slapstick comedy, and all chaos—complete with more than a few spectacular near faceplants that had everyone clutching their sides with laughter.

Picture this: crab ball stance — kiddos sit on their bottoms, palms and feet flat on the ground. The whistle blows, and a dozen kids launch into crab mode, legs flailing, arms wobbling, backs stiff as a board, walking on their hands and feet like little crabs freshly scooped from the ocean. They can take three steps in any direction before passing the ball.

Strategy?

Pass and score.

Simple.

On defense, it's a chaotic scramble to steal the ball—arms flailing, legs kicking—as everyone desperately tries not to faceplant.

Picture a dozen tiny crabs scuttling frantically, bumping into each other, legs tangling, and every so often pausing mid-game to readjust their crab stance or let out an exasperated sigh.

Watching this pack of pint-sized crustaceans chase a ball is equal parts adorable and hilarious—almost like a dozen tiny human bumper buggies in a frantic, sideways dance. They bounce off each other, limbs flailing wildly, struggling to keep balance while chasing a rogue ball that seems to have a mind of its own.

Every collision triggers a symphony of giggles, protests, and the occasional, "Hey! Watch it!"

It's chaos, sure—but the kind that leaves everyone breathless, grinning, and ready to do it all over again.

Apparently, twenty minutes is an eternity in crab ball — long enough for legs to wobble, arms to lose feeling, and for at least three players to debate whether their crab walk qualifies as "advanced" or just "awkward."

Juice break — Capri Suns all around. Fuel for the little critters, recharging their crab legs and refilling their giggle tanks before the chaos resumes.

Then there's "chain reaction," where the real test isn't speed but how quickly you can pass a hand squeeze down a line without getting totally derailed by a full-on giggle attack.

Here's the setup: two lines of kids, a ball at one end, colored cards at the other. I call out a color, they scan their cards, then squeeze the hand of the person behind them. That squeeze sets off a ripple down the line until the last kid grabs the ball.

First team to snag it wins.

Simple, right?

Until the giggles kick in.

One afternoon during chain reaction, everything was humming along—squeezes zipping down the line like a well-oiled machine. Then, right in the middle of the red team's run, little Miguel got distracted by a fly buzzing near his ear. Instead of passing the squeeze, he started swatting at thin air, sending the ripple off course.

Next thing you know, the squeeze arrives at Sofia's hand—who had no clue what was happening—and she burst into giggles. That sparked a full-blown laugh attack down the line. By the time the last kid grabbed the ball, everyone was doubled over—some clutching their sides, others wiping tears from their eyes.

It was less "chain reaction" and more "chain distraction," but honestly, those moments made the game worth playing.

On Wednesdays, "relay kickball" took center stage. The contest of all contests (at least for the kiddos). Think kickball, but with extra bases, extra chaos, and definitely extra yelling.

Relay kickball is kickball's wild cousin. In regular kickball, one kid kicks the ball and the defense tries to get them out.

Yawn, right?

Relay kickball cranks up the chaos: once the ball is kicked, the entire defense has to 1) retrieve it, 2) form a line, and 3) "relay" the ball hand-to-hand down the line to record the out. Meanwhile, the kicker keeps running, scoring a point for every base they safely touch before the out is made.

Here's the twist: if the relay breaks or the ball gets dropped, the defense has to start the whole relay back at square one. It's like a game of hot potato meets track and field—with a dash of yelling for good measure.

The whistle blew, and the game was on. Red vs Blue. Marcos stepped up and smacked the ball with all his might, sending it bouncing toward the far fence. The defense sprang into action like a pack of startled meerkats.

Step one: retrieve the ball. Christian dove, missed, and ended up rolling into the miniature soccer goal.

Step two: form a line. The kids scrambled to get in order—some facing the wrong way, others bumping into each other like bumper cars at a county fair.

Step three: start the relay. The ball flew from hand to hand, but about halfway down the line, little Rosa's grip faltered. The ball slipped and bounced off her elbow, skittering onto the grass.

"Back to the start!" someone yelled, and the defense scrambled to begin again. Meanwhile, Marcos was still rounding bases, a grin plastered across his face like he was in a slow-motion victory lap.

Every failed relay sparked a chorus of groans, laughter, and frantic whispers of, "Okay, this time we got it!" The chaos was delicious—equal parts determination, friendly sabotage, and the pure joy of sibling rivalry played out on a makeshift field.

The red squad got flattened by the blue squad, 175 to 126. No biggie. Win or lose, everyone walked away a champion—armed with a well-earned Otter Pop to soothe the battle wounds and sugar-crash the victorious chaos.

Arts and crafts time was the perfect transition—after all the chaos and competition, the kids got juiced up in a way that made hyperactive monkeys look downright sleepy. And as much as we love the energy, no one wanted to recreate the sun inside our little space.

The kiddos didn't just make art—they lived it. Sometimes they even wore it. One thing was for sure: it all went home with them. That summer, we made paper-mâché piggy banks of every color, size, and shape you could imagine.

Our local credit union kindly donated rolls of quarters so the kids could fill their banks with some serious pocket change.

We crafted hand puppets from brown paper bags and colorful felt. My favorite was an elaborate peacock created by the shyest little human you'd ever meet—so quiet, you'd swear she was the puppet herself.

The kids' favorite?

Flubber.

Not so much for the parents, who spent the week chasing that gooey menace out of clothes, hair, and every nook and cranny imaginable.

Flubber—think of it as the lovechild of glue and a chemistry experiment gone slightly rogue. It's gooey, squishy, and somehow manages to slip through the tiniest cracks like it's got a personal vendetta against your floor.

Watching the kids make it was like witnessing a sticky, slimy symphony of chaos: hands dipped in, swirling, squishing, and occasionally flicking blobs across the room as if trying to start a gooey Jackson Pollock movement.

Every batch came with a warning label in invisible ink: "Will stick to everything but the container." Shirts became walking science projects, hair turned into gelatinous sculptures, and the phrase "Not in your hair!" was shouted at least thirty-seven times before snack break.

Midway through Flubber-making, little Rosa got a bit too enthusiastic. She flicked a glob with the precision of a seasoned artist—but instead of landing in a bowl, it flew straight onto Mr. Velez's—yep, my—baseball cap. There it stuck, wobbling like a jellyfish doing the cha-cha.

I froze for a second, then burst out laughing as the kids pointed and giggled. "Looks like I'm officially part of the art now," I said, peeling the wobbling blob off my hat before it turned into a permanent accessory.

From that moment on, Flubber wasn't just a craft—it was a full-contact, slapstick masterpiece.

Pool days are always a hit. I mean, who doesn't love getting drenched and walking around smelling like chlorine all day? It's the unofficial scent of summer chaos—and the kids wear it like a badge of honor.

But the real highlight of the summer? The visit from the fire department. What started as a straightforward lesson on fire and water safety quickly turned into a full-blown spectacle, complete with suits, a shiny fire truck, and wailing sirens that had the kids' eyes as wide as saucers.

Then came the unexpected twist—a tug-of-war challenge: 20 munchkin campers versus eight confident firefighters. Spoiler alert: those eight fine men seriously underestimated the power of a bunch of sugar-fueled kids.

The firefighters pulled and strained, muscles bulging, but the kids—well, let's just say those little monkeys weren't going anywhere. Not an inch. Not a millimeter. The firefighters were left tugging on air while the kids stood their ground like tiny, determined warriors.

It wasn't even close. And somewhere in the back, I swear I heard the fire chief mutter, "Next time, bring backup."

As a wet reward for their triumph, the kids basked in the cool spray of the firehoses—grinning from ear to ear, drenched and triumphant, soaked in victory and the unmistakable scent of summer fun. (Sorry, parents—definitely not a planned wet day…)

Mealtime was the one moment the kiddos behaved like actual humans—well, as normal as a bunch of sugar-fueled kids can be.

Our Neighborhood House provided lunch, and this wasn't your run-of-the-mill cafeteria fare. We're talking handmade hamburgers with crispy fries and fresh fruit, tender baked chicken with creamy mashed potatoes, savory carne asada with fluffy rice, classic spaghetti and meatballs, and, as a special treat, the kitchen staff showed up one day to help the kids make their own French bread pizzas—messy, fun, and totally worth the extra cleanup.

And so it went… five days stretched into two weeks, and before we knew it, summer was gone.

Those whirlwind weeks of laughter, chaos, and unexpected friendships slipped by faster than anyone wanted.

The community center slowly returned to its usual rhythm—no more paint-splattered tables, no more crab-walking chaos, no more tiny hand squeezes ricocheting down the lines. But the echoes of those summers—sticky fingers, triumphant grins, and the smell of sun and chlorine—lingered long after the last kid went home.

In the end, it wasn't just a day camp; it was a small, messy, joyful celebration of childhood itself.

Definitely not your typical summer camp—but then again, that's what made it unforgettable.

The Quiet Rituals of Becoming

The Quiet Rituals of Becoming

Growing up in those years between pre-teen and teen was like stepping onto a moving escalator that you hadn't asked to ride. One day, you were twelve, sneaking popsicles from the freezer without thinking twice, your knees scraped from endless games of street baseball.

The next, you were thirteen, standing in the hallways of junior high with the unfamiliar weight of a locker combination in your pocket, trying not to trip over your own elbows as the world seemed to have gotten taller overnight.

Junior high was a transitional laboratory, testing everything: your friendships, your courage, your sense of humor. Voices changed, awkwardness multiplied, and suddenly you were hyper-aware of every hair out of place, every note passed too loudly across the room, every misstep that might define you forever—or at least until lunch period.

High school didn't make things simpler—it made them bigger. Larger hallways, louder lockers slamming, more eyes noticing, more rules to navigate. Every new class felt like a separate universe, each teacher an alien entity with unknown laws, and every misstep carried the thrilling terror of discovery.

You were growing up, inch by inch, and every small success—a completed homework assignment, a joke landed without humiliation, a friendship maintained—felt monumental.

High school was less a collection of classes and more a long hallway of rituals no one warned you about. Not fancy ceremonies—more like chaotic, dusty, sweat-soaked ones where the dress code was usually whatever your mom found on sale at Mervyn's or K-Mart.

You didn't have to sign up for them—they signed up for you. One day you were just some kid trying to survive Algebra; the next, you were suddenly expected to run a mile in August heat as if that were a normal way to measure personal worth.

In Calexico, the heat alone was a rite of passage. But these rituals shaped us all, whether we were ready or not.

The first rite most of us tripped into—sometimes literally—was playing a sport. It didn't matter which one. At some point every kid in Calexico found themselves on a field or a court wondering who invented running drills and why they hated teenagers so much.

Everyone had to take P.E., but for some of us that wasn't enough—we voluntarily joined an organized sport, signing up for extra sweat and emotional damage.

The grass during P.E. always smelled like dry earth and sunburn. Your shoes slapped against the fading lines of the field while the coach's whistle cut through the heat like a mosquito you couldn't swat.

I remember one kid collapsing onto the grass after the warm-up lap—the warm-up lap—gasping, "Is this… the whole sport?" Coach didn't blink. "That was just the appetizer." No one laughed because we were all too busy trying to remember what breathing felt like.

During water breaks, someone inevitably tried to trade sweat-soaked T-shirts like they were championship memorabilia, while another kid dramatically collapsed in the shade, moaning, "I think I've invented a new kind of fainting." The rest of us alternated between snickering and trying to figure out if we should help—or just survive. But stepping off that field—sweaty, dusty, panting like a busted vacuum cleaner—you carried something with you.

Maybe not skill.

Maybe not coordination.

But definitely a sense that you'd survived something monumental, or at least mildly traumatizing.

Eventually the soreness faded, and you moved on to the next unspoken ritual: covering your textbooks. Back then, your book cover was your identity, and a brown paper grocery bag was your canvas.

The bag smelled faintly of produce and Sunday errands as your mom flattened it across the table like she was about to perform surgery. Kids today have social media pages; we had textbook covers.

"Don't cut it crooked," she'd say.

"I'm not!"

"You already did."

She was right.

Once wrapped, you got to decorate it with the permanent-marker confidence of a future street artist. Doodles scrawled in with a Bic pen, little band logos, balloon letters of your name—each stroke releasing that sweet, headache-inducing Marks-a-Lot scent that somehow felt like adolescence in liquid form. Stickers and the signatures of the people in your ring of influence filled in the gaps.

And then there were those few artists—the Michelangelos of the mesa—who turned an algebra book into full graffiti murals.

One kid tried to draw a perfect lightning bolt across his algebra book and ended up with a permanent-marker explosion that looked more like abstract modern art than math. By the time he slapped tape over it, the book resembled a crime scene—yet somehow, he strutted down the hall proud as if he'd discovered electricity itself.

A couple of months later, the cover was soft as masa, the corner folded up like a tortilla chip, and held together by tape that looked like it had survived a desert storm.

And just when you thought you'd mastered the art of wrapping, the next classroom treasure arrived: the duplo copies—the holy grail of every class. Fresh off the machine, the stack of papers seemed almost magical, still warm from the press, edges crisp and perfectly aligned. The moment the teacher set them on the desk, every kid in the room leaned in like moths to a flame, holding the paper up to their nose and inhaling deeply.

That smell—hot ink, slightly chemical, and somehow full of possibility—was intoxicating.

It was the smell of being organized, of having something official in your hands, of knowing that today, maybe, you could actually conquer geometry. Fingers lingered along the edges, tapping lightly, flipping the pages with reverence. Some kids even lined them up, carefully separating each copy from the next, like tiny monuments to productivity.

There was always an unspoken race to snag the first copy.

Some kids lurked near the desk like predators, fingers twitching in anticipation. One accidental nudge could send a stack sliding to the floor, papers flying like confetti at a New Year's parade.

Chaos, laughter, and tiny victories marked those brief moments—the closest thing we had to organized sport indoors.

And of course, the social theater of it all—everyone inhaling at once, whispering, "Oh man, it smells so good," or giggling quietly when someone got a nose full of toner dust.

It was fleeting, of course—the scent would fade, the novelty would wear off, and soon enough you'd be scribbling in the margins, doodling on it—but for those first few seconds, it was pure, unsullied joy.

Holding a fresh duplo copy was a tiny, glorious rite of passage, a shared ritual of anticipation and wonder that only existed in the days before PDFs, photocopier apps, and Google Classroom.

And then, inevitably, attention turned to the most delicate of adolescent missions: passing folded notes. Kids today will never know the thrill. A text message? Easy. A note? That was a full covert operation.

The classroom carried that familiar cocktail of pencil shavings, Aqua Net, and impending academic doom. You'd fold the note with precision—square, triangle, or that fancy football fold if you were trying to impress someone. Then you handed it to the bravest kid within reach.

"Pass this to Marisol," you whispered.

"I'm not going over there," he whispered back.

"Please, bro. I'll owe you."

"You already owe me."

Fair point.

Sliding the note across the rows had all the suspense of a telenovela finale. If intercepted? Instant public humiliation. Your social life flashed before your eyes while the teacher cleared her throat dramatically.

A teacher reading your love-sick poem aloud was the 80s version of your text getting screenshotted and shared with the whole school.

“Let’s see what’s so important… shall we read it aloud to the class?”

You learned humility real fast. But if it made it back to you—folded differently—your stomach dropped, your face got hot, and suddenly Algebra didn’t matter. That was our texting. Risky, handwritten, live-or-die romance.

A perfectly folded note wasn’t just communication—it was art. Some kids did the square fold. Some did the triangle. A few geniuses engineered origami masterpieces that opened like treasure maps.

But passing a note was a rite of passage because it was the first time you dared to put your feelings in writing without knowing the outcome. The first time you took a risk—not for grades or sports—but for the possibility of connection.

High school romance was equal parts thrill and terror, usually measured in stolen glances and whispered confessions.

Passing notes might start as covert poetry, but soon you were graduating to full-on strategy: where to meet, when the coast was clear, and how to avoid that one hall monitor with a sixth sense for teenage mischief.

Sometimes a note wasn’t just words—it was coordinates, a secret map to a quick hand-hold behind the bleachers, a rendezvous timed between bells, or an emergency code for a stolen kiss.

Each folded triangle became a miniature blueprint for first love, complete with high-stakes risk and adrenaline in equal measure.

There was an art to sneaking off. Maybe it was the last bell of lunch, when the halls emptied for the library or bathroom breaks, or a quiet corner behind the bleachers where no one thought to look.

The first touch—the light graze of a hand, a foot brushing against yours—felt monumental, a full-on adrenaline spike that made your stomach do somersaults.

"Are you sure no one's coming?"

"I think… yeah… probably… oh God, I hear someone!"

Your hearts raced faster than your sneakers across the cracked asphalt. You didn't need texting, phones, or social media; a quick dash behind the bleachers, a clumsy kiss, and a whispered promise of secrecy was enough.

Every giggle, every bump into each other's arms, felt like an unofficial ceremony, a rite of passage into the world of first love and first heartbreak.

From there, you graduated naturally to the next trial: managing your first locker. It creaked open with the sound of old metal giving up on life. The smell inside was a mix of pencil lead, forgotten gum, and something that might once have been food. You practiced the combination like it was a secret code that unlocked adulthood.

"Left… right… left…"
Click. Nothing.
Try again.
Click. Still nothing.

By the end of week one, you were praying to the locker gods like a pilgrim.

Still, it felt like your territory—one battered little square foot where you could hide a Walkman, a bag of Churritos, the note you were too scared to read, or that referral you got last period but somehow never made it to the office.

Rumors of contraband ran rampant, and random locker searches always loomed like a slow-moving thundercloud.

When they happened, it was never subtle. The assistant principal would appear first, clipboard in hand, eyes narrowing like a hawk spotting its prey. A proctor would trail behind, whistle around their neck, flipping through the hall passes like they were sacred scrolls of doom. "Locker 214," the assistant principal would bark, and you'd feel your stomach do the cha-cha. You had exactly three seconds to pretend your locker was neat, organized, and completely ordinary.

Hands in hair, breath shallow, you'd watch them yank open the metal door with that creak that could announce a robbery to the entire floor. The proctor would rifle through your things with the efficiency of a CIA operative while the assistant principal hovered like a storm cloud, occasionally giving a slow, judgmental nod at a misplaced pencil or a suspiciously crumpled bag of chips.

Every tiny item suddenly felt like evidence, every crumpled note a potential felony.

Once, a classmate's pen exploded mid-combination, sending blue ink across homework and a bag of chips alike. The assistant principal gave a slow nod, as if to say, "You've failed civilization itself," while we all scrambled to clean the mess, half panicked, half laughing.

And even after they left, the echoes of their footsteps seemed to cling to the hallway like a bad perfume. The threat of the next random search hung in the air, invisible but undeniable, a constant reminder that your little kingdom of Churritos, folded notes, and battered Walkman in that locked metal box was fragile, temporary, and fiercely yours—at least until the assistant principal or a proctor decided otherwise.

That fragile sense of independence carried over naturally to Driver's Ed, where they handed you the keys to a car that smelled like panic, vinyl, and 800 previous teenagers who slammed the brakes at the wrong time. The instructor rode shotgun, gripping that emergency brake like a man clinging to his last shred of sanity.

"Check your mirrors," he'd mutter.

"I am!"

"No, you don't need to turn up the radio!"

You learned quickly that adulthood wasn't about driving—it was about managing other people's blood pressure. Passing that final test felt like earning your freedom.

Driving to school with the windows down, blasting your favorite station, air whipping around—nothing felt more adult than that.

And let's be honest… for many students, Driver's Ed wasn't the first time behind the wheel. A good chunk of the population had been driving without a license since junior high. Some because their parents were liberal and allowed it. Others because they stole—err, borrowed—their parents' car and took it for joyrides.

One kid in the next car managed to sideswipe a cone, spin in a perfect circle, and stop just short of a curb—look of triumph on his face, while the instructor's scream echoed down the lot. We laughed, tried to copy, and immediately failed spectacularly, learning both humility and the limits of teenage bravado.

By the time you had your license—or borrowed your parents'—the school parking lot became your first true kingdom. The lot itself was a landscape of possibility, asphalt glowing under the mid-morning sun, dotted with dents, mismatched hubcaps, and the faint, lingering smell of exhaust mixed with tire rubber.

Every vehicle was a statement, a personality, a rolling declaration of independence. A beat-up Chevy Nova whispered, I don't care, but I look cool doing it. A freshly waxed Cutlass said, I have parents with taste—and a little money.

Free periods were sacred. That was the time when rules blurred, the bell didn't dictate life, and the parking lot became an open stage for plotting, hanging out, or just cruising the lot in circles, revving engines like you were auditioning for a Fast and Furious prequel.

Students leaned against hoods, music blasting from cassette decks, arguing about who could do the best burnout—or who had the freshest mix tape.

There was magic in the freedom to come and go, to slip out of class without the world collapsing, to drive with the windows down, wind whipping your hair, radio blasting, knowing that for that one hour—or sometimes thirty glorious minutes—you were the master of your own schedule. It didn't matter that half of us weren't supposed to have a license yet. The lot didn't judge. The lot didn't care. The lot was yours.

Even the tiniest rituals—swapping rides, giving someone a lift to grab lunch at the corner taco stand, or racing to see who could snag the best parking spot—felt like a declaration:

I exist.

I'm independent.

I'm here.

For a teenager, that asphalt kingdom, with its heat, noise, and smell of freedom, was nothing short of paradise.

Skipping school wasn't about rebellion—it was about freedom.

The bell that normally dictated life could be ignored for a morning of conspiracy and adventure. Sometimes it was an art form: slipping out during P.E., ducking behind the cafeteria, pretending you were going to the library when in fact the corner taco stand awaited.

The air outside smelled different than inside—dry, sunbaked asphalt and faint exhaust fumes, as if the world itself had opened a secret door for you. You could sit on the curb, a bag of fries in hand, laughing at your audacity, while algebra homework sulked inside the classroom.

Sometimes the risk was half the fun. You'd return later, trying to look casual, stomach jittery from both tacos and guilt, hoping the teacher didn't notice. The thrill wasn't just the act—it was the feeling that, for a few hours, you were truly in charge of your day, even if just barely.

From asphalt freedom to hairstyles, nothing could humble you faster than the yearbook photo that came months later. You could gel your hair, iron your shirt, stand up straight, promise yourself you wouldn't blink—and somehow, the camera caught you mid-blink, mid-breath, mid-awkward-growth-spurt. Proof, forever, that puberty is undefeated.

Dig out an 80s yearbook and you'll witness the Aquanet Revolution in all its crunchy, wind-resistant glory. Hair wasn't just hair back then—it was a monument to ambition, defiance, and pure teenage stubbornness.

Bangs were teased to skyscraper heights, strands teased, combed, and sprayed into oblivion until they practically defied gravity. Every flick of a head sent a puff of aerosol into the room, leaving a faint chemical halo over your locker and a lingering perfume that clung for days.

Layered cuts stuck out at impossible angles, curling and flipping in ways that made physics scream. Feathered hair flowed like liquid plastic, sides pricked up with hairspray until they could have served as emergency flags in case of a desert rescue.

Even the quiet kids got in on it, somehow managing to make every single strand of their hair declare, I am here, I exist, and yes, I will not bend for you.

And the smell—oh, the smell. A heady mix of lacquer, sweat, and ambition. You could identify a hallway just by the faint buzz of hairspray settling into the fluorescent-lit air.

One wrong move near a group of freshly-sprayed heads and you were instantly dusted in a fine mist of chemically-enhanced rebellion.

It wasn't vanity—it was armor. The higher you teased it, the safer you felt from ridicule. The stickier and stiffer the layers, the closer you were to becoming untouchable. Every photo, every yearbook smile, captured the essence of a generation that treated hairspray like a survival tool.

Wind?

Rain?

A passing bus?

Nothing could touch those meticulously sculpted crowns—they were the ultimate statement of teenage defiance in motion.

Sometimes, the Aquanet-soaked bangs got caught in a P.E. sweatband or poked the passenger next to you during a parking lot cruise, proving that teenage armor could be both spectacular and inconvenient.

Finally, just when you thought you'd mastered the ecosystem, the calendar rolled around to back-to-school shopping—another rite wrapped in polyester and price tags.

The department stores smelled like new cotton and possibilities. You grabbed jeans you hoped would change your entire personality, only to have your mom flip the tag and say, "Ay mijo… absolutely not."

"But everyone has these!"

"Well, go borrow theirs."

Negotiations continued. By the end, compromise meant slightly different socks, but you strutted out like you'd won a minor battle in an invisible war against fashion tyranny.

That first-day outfit—the crisp shirt, the unscuffed sneakers—made you stand a little taller until at least third period, when someone spilled chocolate milk in your general direction.

Nothing marked the transition toward adulthood like your first paycheck. Mine came from a tiny corner store where the register smelled faintly of spilled soda and floor polish.

The uniform was itchy, the name tag impossible to keep straight, but somehow, it made you feel like a miniature adult—official, trusted, and entirely responsible for something that wasn't just homework.

Early mornings smelled of fresh bread, coffee, and the faint panic of stock shortages. You learned quickly that customers were unpredictable, the manager was a human tornado of instructions, and the clock ticked at a pace that made school feel like recess.

"Can you bag these?"

"Yes, ma'am!"

One accidental spill or missed price tag felt catastrophic, but your first paycheck—the crumpled bills, the worn coins—was pure empowerment. That

first taste of real money could buy candy, music, or something utterly frivolous, yet it carried a weight no allowance ever did: the understanding that you had actually done something, somewhere, for someone else—and got paid for it.

One customer demanded exact change for a soda and a pack of gum, eyes narrowing as if my failure would personally destroy her afternoon.

I fumbled, apologized, and somehow survived, walking home with my first paycheck feeling both heroic and dangerously competent.

Looking back, none of these rites were official. No ceremonies, no certificates, no cap and gown. Just sweat, marker fumes, folded notes, awkward dances, and a few half eaten bags of churritos forgotten in a locker.

But each one nudged us forward, taught us something, held us together, made us laugh, made us cringe, made us grow.

And through it all, there was this constant pull to figure things out, to take apart the world piece by piece, to test the limits of what could be done without being caught.

High school never told us these were rites of passage.

But we lived them.

Survived them.

And somehow—miraculously—came out the other side with stories worth telling.

Mischief Monkeys

Mischief Monkeys

Every kid, no matter the generation, knows mischief. It's written deep in our DNA—the most primal way we learn as humans. It's how we explore, how we test boundaries.

It's life itself—the spark that makes each day worth living, memories in the making. Mischief isn't just the big moments; it's the stuff in between the usual kid stuff—the flavor, the spice that turns ordinary afternoons into unforgettable adventures.

At first, it's the little stuff—the harmless trouble parents almost wink at. Sneaking an extra cookie before dinner, making a face behind your teacher's back. It's safe, almost necessary—a kind of practice ground for bigger adventures.

Parents sometimes encourage it, knowingly or not. A sly smile when you push just enough, a story told with laughter about their own youthful escapades. It's their way of passing down the spark—reminding you mischief isn't just rebellion; it's a rite of passage.

These small moments build your confidence, teach you where the edges are, and how far you can stretch before the consequences catch up. It's all part of the messy, wonderful journey toward figuring out who you are.

But what drives kids to dive headfirst into mischief?

Peer pressure—the dare that starts with a nudge and ends in nervous laughter.

Wild ideas hatched from boredom, crazy schemes that make perfect sense only to a kid fueled by sugar and the need to prove something.

A reckless mix of bravery and stupidity, resulting in scraped knees and legendary stories.

Yup, all of the above.

And sometimes, it's Dad's fault—the greatest Mischief Monkey of all. He lives his wild days again through his kids. But don't be fooled: when Mom finds out, he'll throw you under the bus faster than you can say, "I didn't do it!"

Moms get in on the action too, but they're much more discreet.

Through it all, three influencers watch your every move: two perched on your shoulders, whispering encouragement and warnings, and one, ever-present but hidden, offering only a quiet place to mourn and confess (or just lick your wounds).

The right monkey—the spirit of your friends, siblings, cousins. They want you to do it. They cheer you on, reminding you of the legend you're about to become. *What could go wrong?*

The left monkey—visions of Mom and Grandma, the arm of righteousness. They hover, clutching rosaries, pleading, "Por el amor de Dios… please don't."

And the ever-present guy in the mirror—a reflection of you, nothing more. There to hold your regret after the deed is done. The most worthless, valuable person you'll ever have: your guilt, your moral compass, your reminder that, yup, that was a dumbass move. *What's your excuse now? Go talk to Mom…*

And at the center of it all?

You. All grins and jittery nerves, fueled by way too much sugar and wild dreams, itching to prove yourself, outdo your siblings, and carve your own legend—all without actually killing yourself. (Minor injuries? Trophies, really. Battle scars you'd brag about for years.)

Back in the day, these reckless deeds sprouted from endless hangouts, late-afternoon bike rides leaving your legs screaming, and hours chilling outside while grown-ups talked about boring adult stuff.

Maybe it was a way to crack open the boredom of the everyday, to kick-start a new adventure—one you hoped didn't end with a trip to the emergency room or, worse, explaining to Mom why you looked like a human pincushion.

There was David's legendary walk across the top of the brick wall separating our house from the neighbor's—a narrow ledge barely wider than your sneakers. The wall itself wasn't the most structurally sound structure. It had a slight lean toward our house and a bit of a wobble.

On one side, the neighbor's rottweiler—a bark so terrifying it could wilt a cactus—lunging as if you were the greatest threat to humanity. On the other side, my mom's penca de nopales, those prickly cactus pads perfectly designed to punish any poor soul foolish enough to fall. Either way, the landing was going to hurt.

Then came the shaky bike ramp, a masterpiece of engineering made from thirty bricks and an old ironing board "borrowed" from the laundry room. It was known as *La Rampa.* Heart pounding, you'd pedal with everything you had and launch into glory—or crash spectacularly, earning a chorus of "¡Ay, mijo!" from the sidelines.

Who could forget the legendary Jimmy and his corner shop? The mission wasn't just to snag a bag of chips—it was to pull it off right under Ole Jimmy's hawk eyes. The guys in our Boy Scout troop had this ongoing dare—one of us eventually had to succeed in snagging something out from Ole Jimmy.

One kid tried the "chaos and confusion" approach, toppling a pyramid of soda cans in a glorious, carbonated avalanche. The distraction lasted all of three seconds before Jimmy's glare cut through the air like a machete through warm butter.

Busted!

No need to call the cops—Ole Jimmy's justice was swifter and far more terrifying. He'd lock the store, march you home by the ear, and deliver the news with the grim authority of a man reading your obituary: "Your mom's gonna hear about this."

And then there was the butterfly knife—our own Excalibur of poor decisions. We'd practice flipping it open with all the swagger of a spaghetti western hero, except our "gunslinger" moves usually ended in something closer to a blooper reel. Band-aids became less of a medical necessity and more of a fashion statement.

"Watch this!" my brother declared once, chest puffed out, as his audience of equally reckless friends leaned in, equal parts impressed and concerned. The blade would twirl, click, and—oops—nearly separate him from a fingertip. Spoiler: he almost never nailed it, but he did collect something even more valuable than skill—a nice little set of scars. You know, as proof he "lived to tell the tale."

One day, after he and I had argued about… actually, I don't remember what we argued about. But he took a fighting stance, hollered "¡A ver pues, cabrón!" and flipped that blade open in one swift and smooth motion. Perfect form. So perfect, he shocked himself right out of whatever anger he had. We both ended up laughing.

"How'd you do that?"

"Don't know!" he said with a shrug.

Ah, the trials and tribulations of being brothers.

The bravest of all? The tequila swig challenge. Whoever could take a swig of Tata's tequila without wincing was king of the night—until the burning took over and you begged for water. Nobody ever admitted how bad it really hurt.

This was everyday kid stuff. Yeah, the scoldings stung—Mom's voice echoing like a warning siren—but no matter what, you'd strut back to the crew, ready to tell the tale of how you survived, maybe exaggerating a little. The lucky ones were never caught, and those stories became legends.

Oh, how those legends grew—retold at family reunions with cousins laughing till their sides hurt, adults nodding in disbelief but laughing along, secretly wishing they had the guts to do the same.

Sure, there were more sinister things—at least that's how parents saw it. Trouble that earned extra scoldings, grounded weekends, or the dreaded "Wait till your father gets home" warning whispered like a curse.

Maybe it was the time the neighbor's car got mysteriously covered in shaving cream, or the time the cops showed up to scold us for shooting pigeons with a BB gun. Those moments weren't just mischief—they were borderline legend, the kind that made your heart race long after the fact.

My older sister Norma always claimed she was "the good one," but the summer she discovered her window could slide open just far enough for her to slip out, that title… wobbled a little.

It happened on one of those dead-still Calexico nights when even the crickets were too lazy to chirp. The rest of us were asleep, dreaming innocent dreams, while Norma—restless, seventeen, and craving freedom—lifted her window, slid out, and tiptoed across the front yard like a burglar in her own home.

Dad's 1965 Dodge Dart waited in the driveway, steel bumpers glinting under the streetlight like old battle armor. Norma slid behind the wheel, turned the key, and felt the engine rumble to life. Maybe she imagined a whole world cracking open in front of her—late-night adventures, music blasting, the sweet taste of rebellion.

And then, in her excitement to flee the scene, she forgot one tiny, crucial detail: steering.

Instead of backing out gracefully into the street, she reversed in a perfectly straight line—straight into Uncle Tommy's pride and joy, his 1981 Chevy Monte Carlo. The crunch was loud enough to wake the birds up in Yuma. The dent in the Monte Carlo was big enough to hide in.

Norma froze. The party was definitely over.

Heart pounding, she pulled the Dart back into the driveway like nothing had happened. She inspected the bumper—nothing. Not a scratch. That old Dart was a tank; Uncle Tommy's Monte Carlo didn't stand a chance.

She slipped back inside, set her alarm for 5:00 a.m., and tried to sleep, probably still tasting the dust of near-disaster.

At dawn sharp, she waltzed into Mom's room, shaking her awake.

"Mamá… creo que escuché un ruido fuerte afuera."

Mom didn't even open her eyes. "No te preocupes. Ya que llegue tu papá del trabajo revisará qué fue. Duérmete."

Around 6:30am, Dad came home from the water treatment plant, still wearing the faint smell of chlorine and desert air. Mom poured him his coffee and set toast in front of him, spread with the usual peach marmalade. She told him what Norma had reported.

Dad took a bite of his toast, took his cup of joe with him, sipping as he walked out to the front.

When he returned, he took another bite of toast and asked my mom for another cup of coffee.

"¿Encontraste algo?" she asked.

Dad shrugged. "No. Pero parece que le chocaron el carro a Tomás."

Mom blinked. "¿Qué?"

"Sí. Está chocado. Tiene un golpe del lado del chofer."

Mom shook her head. "Eso ha de haber sido lo que escuchó la Norma."

And that was that.

Norma, sitting at the breakfast table with the face of a saint and the guilt of a felon, just nodded solemnly, like she was grateful the neighborhood hadn't burned down in the night.

No one ever found out the truth.

Well… until now.

If Norma was the midnight ninja of unauthorized car usage, my brother Harvey was the exact opposite. He preferred daylight—bold, loud, and impossible to miss. Subtlety was not his native language.

The first time he tried to take one of the family vehicles, he chose Dad's work truck. In broad daylight. On a Saturday. With everyone home. Because of course.

He hopped in like he owned the place, turned the key, grinned that mischievous grin of his… and promptly discovered he wasn't quite tall enough to see out the back window.

Attempt #1: reverse, *crunch*, right into the palm tree.

Attempt #2, because apparently the lesson still hadn't downloaded: reverse, *CRUNCH*, into the same palm tree—this time with more speed, more confidence, and a much louder sound that probably echoed across the neighborhood.

The steel rear bumper was bent, the palm tree had a dent in it—an actual dent in a tree—and the evidence was as undeniable as the desert sun.

Dad found out. How could he not? The tree looked like it had been in a bar fight.

Do I remember the consequence? No. Or maybe I don't want to.

Harvey should've retired right then, but no—he had a flair for sequels.

The second incident has grown into legend, retold in our family like a myth whispered around campfires. This time he took Mom's 1979 Thunderbird—powder blue, long, wide, and way too elegant for whatever he and his friends had planned.

The story goes they drove all the way to San Diego and back, three idiots on an odyssey. They made it almost home—almost—before running out of gas four miles outside Calexico.

Somehow, they managed to find gas, refill the Thunderbird, and return it to the driveway like nothing happened, dust settling around it like the end of a Western.

Ask Harvey about it today and he'll shrug, smile, and give you one of those "well, you know…" looks.

The details?

The truth?

Only he knows for sure. (I'm pretty sure God has the receipts too.)

Wild and reckless as they were, those moments helped shape who we became. Lessons about limits, consequences, and the rush of stepping just a little too far outside the lines. Mischief wasn't just trouble; it was the messy, imperfect workshop where we built courage, creativity, and stories worth telling.

Honestly, some of those "sinister" escapades probably saved us from being boring adults. Because the best legends always come with scratches, raised eyebrows, and stories that get better every time they're told.

Today, social media has turned mischief into a spectacle. Back then, what we did wasn't always safe—maybe a flicker of pyromania, maybe a prank that made neighbors clutch their pearls—but it was all good-natured.

Just kids testing limits, making our own rules, writing stories no one else could tell. No likes, no shares, no evidence—just the memory living where it belonged.

Now? Mischief is driven by the hunger for fame, the chase for clicks and likes, and instant viral attention. These aren't simple dares anymore. Sometimes, they're outright death wishes—reckless stunts filmed and uploaded for millions to judge, laugh, or cringe.

The stakes have never been higher. There's no room for second chances when every dumb move is recorded and immortalized online faster than you can say, "What was I thinking?" One slip-up, one bad decision, and your mischief isn't a funny childhood story—it's a viral cautionary tale.

(YOLO, right? Because nothing screams living on the edge like public humiliation.)

And yet, that primal urge?

Still kicking like a toddler hyped up on three cups of soda.

That itch to sneak out, push boundaries, and test Mom's patience?

It's just found a new stage—with unlimited views, instant judgment, and a comment section full of keyboard warriors ready to roast you.

So how do we hold onto the spirit of mischief—the joy, the learning, the bonding—without becoming internet legends for all the wrong reasons?

Maybe it's time for a new kind of courage: being mischievous off-camera, testing limits with common sense, and remembering the best stories aren't the ones that rack up likes, but the ones told around campfires, whispered at sleepovers, or rehashed at family reunions when everyone's had a few too many.

But hey, the world's still watching, inventing new ways to "top that." Even adults have jumped in—posting wild stunts, chasing likes like kids chasing glory.

And those three classic influencers?

They're right there with you, scrolling and snickering:

That guy in the mirror, shaking his head like, "Really? Again?"

The right monkey, cheering, "Go big or go home, baby!"

And the left monkey? Still clutching rosaries, whispering, "Por el amor de Dios, please don't."

The more things change, the more they stay the same.

Mischief's just got a bigger audience—and an embarrassingly long memory.

That One Time at Band Camp

That One Time, At Band Camp

I didn't exactly *choose* the band life; the band life kind of chose me.

Back in middle school, my social calendar consisted of exactly two things: tagging along with my older sister to football games, and pretending not to stare at the high schoolers like they were celebrities-especially the girls in the drill team (*blush*).

My sister was in Drill—hair perfect, uniform pressed, like she was one pep rally away from getting her own TV show. Her boyfriend played trumpet in the band, and he carried himself like a guy who knew he had the loudest instrument on the field.

Watching them from the bleachers, something clicked. The lights. The cheering. The music floating over the warm Calexico night. The band looked like they were in on some secret—like they belonged to something. And I wanted in.

So one afternoon, I picked up an old trumpet—dented, missing a valve cap, probably older than I was—and started messing around. At first it sounded like a dying duck. Maybe a duck with allergies. But then, slowly, those awkward squeaks turned into notes. Notes turned into scales. And next thing you know, I wasn't just making noise—I was playing *music.*

By freshman year, I'd joined the band officially.

Suddenly I had rehearsals, section leaders, competitions, early mornings that felt more like late nights, and a new sense of identity: Band Kid.

And that opened the door to a whole series of moments—some heroic, some embarrassing, all unforgettable.

And one of the first moments that proved band life was going to be anything but predictable happened under the bright stadium lights on a Friday night.

Freshman year.

First Varsity home game of the year.

Calexico vs. Brawley—one of those rivalries where even the concession stand ladies got fired up. The stadium lights were buzzing, the bleachers packed, and the whole town felt like it had squeezed itself onto those metal seats.

We had rehearsed a beautiful arrangement of the Star-Spangled Banner—trumpet solo up front, band providing those rich bass harmonies behind it. The kind of version that made people stand a little taller and maybe wipe a tear if they were feeling dramatic.

The spotlight was meant for our senior soloist. This guy had the résumé: three years of marching, slicked-back hair, and the kind of confidence that usually filled a football field. Usually.

The drum roll began—steady, powerful, like a heartbeat waking up the entire stadium.

Rrrrrrrrrrrrrrrrrrrroll...

The cue hit.

And… nothing.

No trumpet.

No opening note.

Just the drumline rumbling and a whole town collectively leaning forward like, “Uhh…?”

I glance left, and there he is—horn up, eyes wide, frozen like someone hit pause. Stage fright, panic, spiritual crisis—I don’t know. But he wasn’t playing.

And nobody else was about to move.

The entire trumpet section suddenly found their shoes very interesting.

I don’t know what came over me. Maybe adrenaline. Maybe teenage stupidity. Maybe the ghost of John Philip Sousa himself whispering, “Do it, kid.”

To hell with it.

I stepped out of formation, marched straight toward the fifty-yard line—right into the spotlight that wasn’t meant for me—and raised my horn like I owned the place.

And I let that first note fly.

A clean, bold, “seasoned-veteran-who?” kind of opening.

BOOM.

The band snapped in on cue like they’d been waiting for me the whole time.

Just like that, the anthem soared across Calexico High’s Willis Ward Field, and for the next minute and a half, I wasn’t a scared freshman. I was *the* trumpet player.

When it ended, there was this ripple of unexpected applause—people clapping not because they had to, but because something wild and unscripted had just happened. Even the rival fans looked impressed, which is saying something.

I looked up at Mr. Williams—the band director: Two-handed thumbs up. The universal sign for "I don't know what you just did, but I'm glad you did it."

And from that night on, things were… different.

The whispers in the band room.

The sudden respect usually reserved for upperclassmen.

"Watch out, Calexico—Mariano has arrived."

Well… maybe not quite. But things did feel different in the horn section.

But as wild as that moment felt, it didn't magically make me some prodigy. Nope—my real climb happened the old-fashioned way: slowly, stubbornly, one practice session at a time.

I wasn't the most gifted musician. Hell, I hadn't even touched a horn before freshman year. Reading music? Barely. Sight-reading? Forget it. But I had one skill: I could *parrot*. Play a tune a couple of times, and I could mimic it perfectly.

So, I practiced. *Relentlessly.*

I carried my music everywhere—classrooms, lunch tables, the living room—reviewing fingerings like a mad scientist studying formulas. Sometimes I'd get in trouble for singing the notes aloud during class. Once. Twice. Ten times. Who was counting? My teachers, probably.

At home, after homework and chores, I played until my mom would storm in to confiscate the horn. I was just too damned loud, too determined to stop. Every squeak, buzz, and off-note was a step closer to mastery—or at least to first chair.

I memorized every piece before anyone else. Every scale, every etude, every finger-busting passage. While the second-chair kid—who swore he didn't even practice—leaned casually on his stand, I was a one-person marching army.

And eventually, all that obsessive, slightly ridiculous practice paid off. First chair. My hands, my ears, my relentless parrot-like memory had done it. I had arrived.

Not with natural talent, not with effortless skill. But with stubbornness, obsession, and enough hours of squeaky, relentless, chaotic practice to fill a small stadium.

And for a scrawny freshman kid with nothing but a horn and a dream?

That was victory.

First chair didn't arrive in a single, glorious "unanimous vote" moment. No, it came quietly, unceremoniously, almost invisibly—through the little daily victories, the stubborn persistence, the obsessive memorization of every note. I learned it all—the first, second, and third trumpet parts—so that when others struggled to sight-read the music (they apparently didn't practice), I could play it on demand, anytime, anywhere.

Day by day, rehearsal by rehearsal, my reliability became impossible to ignore. And one afternoon, almost without ceremony, Mr. Williams handed me the first trumpet parts. The next week, I got them before anyone else. And just like that, no fanfare, no vote, no announcement, I was first chair.

Not because I was the best naturally.

Not because I had talent handed to me.

But because I showed up.

Every. Single. Day.

Obsessed, relentless, and a little ridiculous.

And for a kid who had barely touched a horn before freshman year, that was more than enough.

But band had a way of surprising me just when I thought I'd reached my ceiling.

Right when things felt steady, another opportunity showed up—bigger, louder, and way beyond anything I'd imagined.

My junior year in high school, I was privileged with one of those once-in-a-lifetime moments: performing at the jersey retirement for Padres (and Dodgers) great Steve Garvey at Jack Murphy Stadium. I have absolutely no recollection of how I came to be selected, but I *do* remember getting the sheet music, the stack of extra rehearsals after regular band practice, and the seriousness that came over all of us once we realized, *Wait... this is happening.*

We traveled up on the day of the performance—April 16, 1988—buzzing with equal parts excitement and teenage confusion. When we arrived at The Murph, we were herded deep into the bowels of the stadium, where a couple hundred high school musicians gathered in a not-quite-organized cluster of cases, uniforms, and nervous chatter. Two songs. That's all we had to get right. And somehow, that made it feel even bigger.

After an intense rehearsal, we suited up, straightened shakily-tied neck cords, and lined up. As we moved toward the tunnel, the sound of the crowd grew louder—this swelling roar that made my chest tighten and my trumpet feel like it had suddenly doubled in weight.

Then… showtime.

A block of high school musicians stepped out of the tunnel in right-center field, marching into this massive bowl of noise and glaring stadium lights. The crowd. The nerves. That surreal, gravity-defying moment when you realize you're actually on the field, not watching from the cheap seats.

The percussion section kicked into a cadence as we marched across the grass and stationed ourselves in center field, just behind second base. The stage sat right on the bag itself. And there he was—Steve Garvey in the flesh. No time to gawk or be starstruck. The band director gave the signal, the music started, and muscle memory took over.

Before we knew it, it was done. Another signal. And just like that, we were filing back off the field.

A whole stadium moment—gone in a flash.

But man… what a flash.

And if music gave me some unforgettable memories, it had absolutely nothing on what came next. Because somewhere between rehearsals and performances, life—real life—stepped in with the plot twist of all plot twists.

That same year, I met *the one.*

I'd known of her before that particular day—seen her around, talked to her here and there. She was my brother's age, same graduating class, a freshman. She still brings up the "rock incident" and jokes about how I *meant* to hit her.

Truth is, she was hanging around with my brother and a few others, and I was tossing pebbles at him—you know, because that's what brothers do. And on that day, the baseball player somehow forgot how to aim. Maybe it was divine intervention. Maybe destiny has a wicked sense of humor, but that day, the rocks hit her (allegedly).

It wasn't until months later that things shifted.

She was in band too. Played the clarinet. Who would've guessed that band camp—of all things—would be what brought us together?

Band camp was exactly what you'd expect: two weeks in the summer full of marching basics, music, and the usual nonsense from upperclassmen (mostly the boys). Then came uniform day. Seniors first, then juniors, then sophomores. Freshmen got whatever was left in the "lost causes" section of the instrument room.

I had my uniform at home—never turned it in. Perks of being the band teacher's favorite horn player. (Okay, enough about that.)

I wandered into the instrument room to organize my stuff in my little corner, and that's when I saw her—Lisa. Half-buried in the closet, sighing dramatically with every ill-fitting coat she tried on. So I casually asked, "You need help?"

She stepped back, a little startled. And just like that—she froze. I froze. Both of us paused mid-breath.

The light from the tiny window sliced through the dust hanging in the air and landed right across her face. Her eyes—big, soft brown—caught mine, and for one heartbeat, the rest of the room just… disappeared. The smell of valve oil. The clatter of music stands. The low hum of band-camp chaos faded out like someone slowly turning a volume knob.

Classic teenage magic.

I don't know if she felt the same thing—I've actually never asked her—but I felt everything a smitten boy could feel. And then some.

The rest of that year, the rest of the world blurred whenever she was around. We did the flirty teenage stuff. Passed notes. Held hands. Hung out. Talked about everything and absolutely nothing. Lit up when we saw each other. Football games, winter pep band, parades, McDonald's trips. She'd even show up at my baseball games, pretending it was a coincidence.

And then one day… we kissed.

Totally unplanned.

Completely random.

I'd walked her to her mom's office at the old gym—her mom was the PE teacher. I don't even remember how we ended up on the other side of the gym next to the electrical box, but that spot? That became ours. I turned toward her, she looked up at me, and bam—our lips met. I melted. We pulled back and just stood there, two teenagers giggling like fools.

Later that night, after quinceañera practice, I asked her to be my girlfriend. She cried and said, "I have to ask my mother…"

What's a guy supposed to feel after that?

It was a Friday. We went home. The whole weekend passed with zero contact. Monday morning came; we barely exchanged glances during zero period. After class, I stepped outside for the short break before first-period band… and she appeared behind me.

We locked eyes.

She smiled.

My knees betrayed me.

"That question you asked me… do you remember?" (Of course I remembered—I'd been thinking about it nonstop.) I nodded dumbly.

"My answer is yes."

We kissed. We hugged. And once again, the rest of the world disappeared.

Everything after that felt better—brighter, sharper—simply because I was with her. The only thing that cast a shadow over my teenage joy was the moment I knew would eventually come: meeting her father.

He was a school principal.

Now, I wasn't a troublemaker, but let's just say principals and I had… history. Not major incidents—just the kind of "frequent flyer" familiarity that makes you instinctively straighten up whenever you see a walkie-talkie and a tie. So naturally, the idea of meeting her principal father terrified me. It felt inevitable, like Thanos snapping half my confidence away.

And then the day came.

He picked us up from school and offered to give me a ride home. I got in the back seat and immediately forgot how to be a functioning human being. I couldn't tell you what he talked about. Could've been sports, school, taxes, the weather—no clue. I was too deep in a fear-induced haze. My survival instincts were on high alert.

But I *do* remember one thing.

Somewhere in the middle of that ride, he looked at me through the rearview mirror and asked, "So… you want to be Lisa's boyfriend?"

Once again, my teenage self betrayed me. No words. No cool, confident answer. Just a dumb nod.

He reached back, shook my hand with this firm, principal-style handshake and said, "I approve."

That was it. No lecture. No rules. No threats about respecting his daughter. Just a handshake that somehow said everything he needed to say. And I exhaled for the first time in ten minutes.

And in case you were wondering—I did say she was "*the one.*"

She was.

She still is.

All these years later, we're married, we've got two incredible kids, and, of course, a dog—because every good love story deserves a loyal sidekick.

And while love was unfolding in its own chaotic teenage way, band kept giving me stories—mostly hilarious ones—whether I asked for them or not.

Funny how the topic of these "experienced' band uniforms keep entering the story.

Our band uniforms were old, but classy—like something pulled straight from a 1960s halftime show and kept alive out of sheer pride and stubbornness. We wore long white overcoats cinched with a maroon belt and a gold buckle that always felt one notch too tight. Each sleeve had a small gold banner embroidered on the shoulder with *Calexico* in maroon thread, the kind of detail you didn't notice until the sun hit it just right.

The maroon pants had a two-inch gold trimmed white stripe running down each leg—bold, clean, unmistakable. White shoes and gloves rounded out the look. And the crown jewel, the thing that made us look both dignified and slightly absurd, was the shako: a tall, fuzzy maroon hat with a sharp white triangle on the front and a gold tassel hanging down like it was trying its best to behave. A little old-school, sure. But when we marched onto a field, we stood out.

And honestly? We looked good doing it.

Given the vintage status of our dress uniforms, there was always a steady comedy of wardrobe malfunctions. Missing buttons, ripped seams, a shako plume that wouldn't stay upright, a zipper that chose violence at the worst possible moment—there was always something. More than one of us survived thanks to a last-minute safety-pin rescue from the pit crew of moms who traveled with us like NASCAR mechanics in sensible shoes.

And our band director? He insisted you still march because "the show must go on," even if your overcoat was holding together by pure willpower and two borrowed pins.

It was chaos. It was ridiculous.

And it was all part of the charm.

This all came to life for me right before a parade in Imperial. We were at the band staging area—tuned up, warmed up, mentally preparing for that long march ahead. Time for one quick run-through of our parade set, then showtime. As squad and section leader, I always marched on the end, the first unlucky soul visible to the spectators on that side.

We lined up.

Band director gave the signal.

Horns up…

That's when I heard it—*and felt it.*

A loud, unmistakable *RIIIIIIIIIIIIIIIP*, followed by the sudden, icy breeze slipping straight down my spine.

Gasps.

Laughter.

Then genuine concern.

I stood there stunned, but honestly? Not entirely surprised. With uniforms that old, it was really just a matter of time. The people behind me said it looked like the entire back of my coat simply *exploded.* All three seams—top to bottom—split wide open. Outer layer, lining…everything. Just shredded fabric flapping in the wind like a broken curtain.

And we had *two minutes* until parade kickoff.

Then came the Band Moms.

They descended on me like a NASCAR pit crew—quick, efficient, slightly terrifying. In 90 seconds flat, they had me spun around, arms out, while about six dozen clothespins, safety pins, and emergency "whatever works" fasteners were clipped across my back. I looked like a science project held together by hope and household hardware.

But it worked.

Thirty seconds later, I was back in formation, pretending I wasn't being held together by the combined power of Elmer's ingenuity and maternal determination.

And the parade marched on.

The following Monday, I found myself performing a little more "bandroom heroics." I liberated someone of their coat because, frankly, it fit me better. I had every right—or at least I thought I did. Surprisingly, no one complained.

Of course, band wasn't the only double life I was living. Sometimes, being a teenager means juggling more identities than you have time or common sense for—and nowhere was that clearer than on Friday nights.

A handful of us played JV football, and we always lived that precarious double life: leaving the JV game halfway through to get ready for band performances at the Varsity games. Sprinting off the field, cleats half-off, shoulder pads flying, friends waiting in the instrument room with uniforms ready like a NASCAR pit crew. Wiping sweat, slapping on gloves, grabbing your horn, and running back out before the drum major even gave the downbeat.

That year's homecoming still stands out. Normally, we had enough time to get cleaned up and into uniform, but homecoming was chaos multiplied—more activities, less time, more eyes. Our JV coach warned us: we had to stay for the whole game. And this was a *game we could actually win.*

Late in the fourth quarter, down by a touchdown. One last running play. Maybe I'd score? Nope. Tackled short of the goal line. Hard hit. I get up, shake my head, and glance at the scoreboard—about a minute left. Coach calls timeout.

Me and another band-playing teammate don't even think. We just… leave. Literally. Left the huddle behind, make a beeline off the field, Jump the fence, haul ass to the band room, still in full football gear.

When we arrive, everyone's staring: *"Dude, where have you been? You smell... awful."*

No time for chit-chat. I'm immediately herded into the instrument room. Band friends go full pit-crew mode: stripping off pads, toweling me down, spraying a little perfume like magic, and shoving me toward the lineup.

Somehow, in record time, I grab my horn, take my place outside, and just like that: pregame and the National Anthem awaited. Cleats gone, pads gone, uniform on, adrenaline through the roof.

And for those few minutes, I was no longer the bruised JV running back—I was a band kid on a mission, and the stadium had no idea the chaos it had just witnessed behind the scenes.

Senior year was more of the same: football games, Lisa, parades, Lisa, halftime shows, Lisa, prom with Lisa… and all the other senior activities the school threw together.

At the annual band awards banquet, I was unanimously awarded the John Philip Sousa Award, given to the best musician in the band. Of course it was me. It was always me.

But in all seriousness, I was humbled. There were plenty of better musicians, but my work ethic put me ahead. I had to work harder. I didn't really know how to read music. My knowledge of music theory was basically zero. But I loved it. I worked at it. And the fact that my peers voted for me spoke more about them than it did about me.

Looking back, all of these moments—big, small, ridiculous, terrifying—stack together into this strange, unforgettable mosaic of who I was becoming.

High school for me was a veritable mish-mash of activity.

I wasn't a popular kid—not by any stretch. But I had friends who played in all the popular circles.

I wasn't a star athlete, but I played sports, suited up, and somehow found myself hanging out with the jocks.

I wasn't a genius, not nerdy-smart, but I did well enough to snag a few academic awards along the way.

I was just a scrawny, scrappy kid who just happened to run the gray areas of every circle that made up high school life. Not quite fitting in, but never fully out of place either.

Except in band.

Band Kid? That was one hundred percent me.

No denying it.

I was the Band Geek—and honestly, I embraced that title before anyone could use it against me. Because for me, that wasn't an insult. That was the heart of my high school experience. The early mornings, the halftime rush, the cracked notes, the uniforms held together by safety pins, the friendships built through rehearsals and road trips—all of it worked. All of it mattered.

And now, all these years later—decades, honestly—I can see just how much those four years shaped me.

The confidence.

The stubbornness.

The willingness to step up when the moment unexpectedly calls your name.

The understanding that belonging doesn't always mean fitting into one place, but finding the place that fits *you.*

Band did that for me.

Band made me.

And I wouldn't change a single off-key, out-of-breath, perfectly imperfect moment of it.

TINKERING:

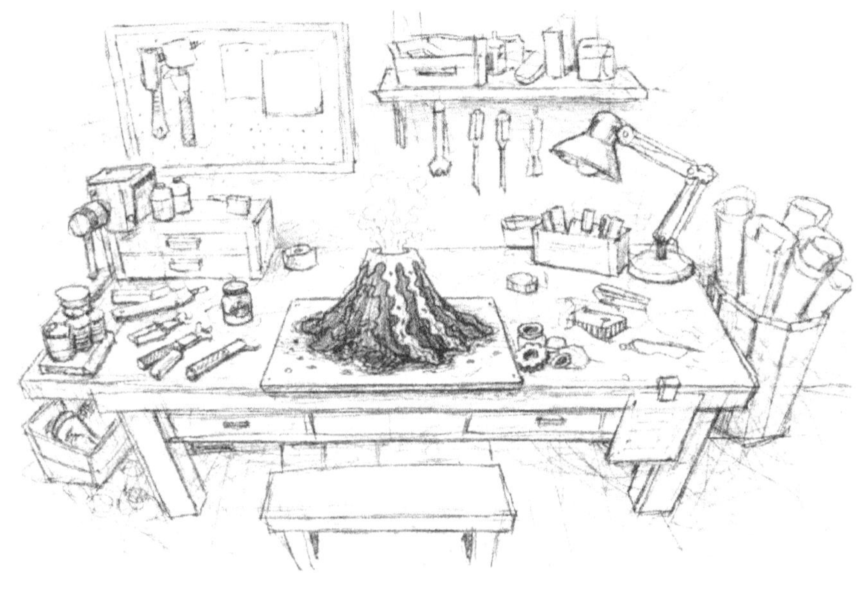

CURIOSITY OR MISCHIEF

Tinkering: Curiosity or Mischief?

Once upon a time, every kid was a tinkerer. We learned by unscrewing things, prying them open, poking around inside. Radios, bikes, door hinges, cassette decks — if it rattled, clicked, or hummed, we had to know why.

There were no YouTube tutorials or step-by-step guides, just a screwdriver, a roll of tape, and an unreasonable amount of confidence. Half the fun was the mystery of whether it would ever work again.

Most of that tinkering happened at home — on kitchen tables, garage floors, and anywhere we could scatter a few screws without getting yelled at. But school chipped in, too, in its own way. The games, the puzzles, the little classroom contraptions and science kits all nudged us to think, to poke, to wonder how things fit together.

Even recess had its own lessons: building forts out of loose cardboard, turning jump ropes into pulley systems, figuring out how to make a marble roll just a little faster.

Somewhere along the way, we traded that kind of exploring for slick gadgets we weren't supposed to open — sealed phones, laptops with warnings about "voiding the warranty." Kids don't get many chances now to see how things actually tick.

I was one of those original tinkerers, and I never outgrew it.

My dad was a bona fide handyman, and his tool shed was a treasure cave — shelves stacked with tools of every size, jars of screws and washers, rolls of wire, scraps of wood, anything that might be useful to build, patch, fix, or restore.

It smelled like sawdust, oil, and a hint of old leather, and the clinking of jars and metal on metal was its own kind of music. It was the closest thing we had to a universe with its own laws. If something broke, the answer was always in there somewhere — you just had to dig, tinker, or improvise your way to it.

That shed is where I learned the sacred rituals of turning something over in your hands, studying its shape, guessing at its purpose, and then testing your theory with a loud click, snap, or sometimes a whoops. My brother and I spent hours sprawled on the garage floor, rolling tiny gears across the concrete like we were surgeons performing delicate operations.

My dad could fix pretty much anything. And if he couldn't figure it out, he'd resort to the art we lovingly called *the chicanada - Mexican Engineering*.

For those not in the know, it's basically engineering with no rules, no guides, no official parts — just whatever was within reach and could be bent, wedged, twisted, or coerced into doing the job. A spoon became a lever, a shoelace a belt, a piece of cardboard a gasket.

"Does this really belong there?" I asked once, holding up a spring that had no obvious purpose.

"Technically? No," Dad said, eyes on the spinning motor. "Practically? Absolutely."

Did it look pretty? Absolutely not.

Did it work? Most of the time.

And when it didn't, well, that's what more chicanadas were for.

My brother and I learned this valuable art, and we put it to the test often. Sometimes under Dad's expert tutelage; most of the time in secret, trying to cover up anything we'd "fixed" beyond its original usefulness — which was often.

As a kid, I'd take apart anything with moving parts: the alarm clock, a blender, the family toaster. I'd spread every screw, spring, and loose part across the table like a tiny army ready for battle, then put it all back together — sometimes with a leftover screw or two.

If it worked, great.

If not, I liked to think it was already doomed before I got my mitts on it.

My bike was the recipient of constant "innovation." That poor thing spent more time flipped upside down in the driveway than actually on the road. Every rattle was an opportunity, every loose bolt a challenge.

We'd jury-rig reflectors with tape, tighten the chain with a flathead that definitely wasn't meant for bikes, and swap out parts from other half-dead bikes we'd scavenged around the neighborhood.

By the time I was done with it, the original factory design was more of a polite suggestion than a blueprint.

"Are you sure that brake lever belongs there?" my brother asked one afternoon.

"Absolutely," I said, brandishing a piece of bent coat hanger. "Physics is a suggestion too."

And always, after any "upgrades" were engineered and installed, a paint job followed. Nothing fancy — usually a few swipes of leftover spray paint or a brush dipped in whatever color we had on hand — but it was our signature, the final flourish that made the bike ours. Sometimes the colors bled together in wild, accidental patterns; sometimes the decals bubbled and peeled like old wallpaper. But to us, it was perfection — proof that we had conquered both mechanics and style, however questionably.

One of the more memorable incidents came the day I decided to operate on a miniature, table-top grandfather clock. I couldn't tell you who it belonged to; it just sat there on a shelf in my grandmother's house, frozen, its little brass hands stuck at some forgotten hour.

Naturally, I saw it as an invitation.

I picked it up, turned it over in my hands, and decided a bit of surgery might bring it back to life. Once I opened the case, I discovered an entire universe inside — gears, springs, levers, all crammed together in precise little rows. There were so many pieces.

Undaunted, I examined each one, set them neatly on the table, and then, with the confidence only a ten-year-old can muster, put everything back where I thought it belonged.

When I finished, there were no leftover parts — a personal best. Success! The only hitch was that I couldn't find the key to wind it.

Improvisation was my specialty, though, so I used a screwdriver to give the spring a few careful turns. To my delight, the clock began to tick. I was positively beaming.

That's when I noticed the hands moving… backward. *Counter-clockwise.*

"Uhm…..shit! What the hell did I do wrong?" I whispered to myself.

Nomido. Too late now. Everyone would be back soon, and can't have them catch me in the act. Time was slipping, fast. (I shall resist the urge to insert a time joke here).

I gave the clock a quick polish, set it back on the shelf as if nothing had happened, and went outside to play. No pasa nada.

No one ever mentioned it, and to this day I have no idea what became of that rebellious little clock.

Part of me likes to think it's still out there, running in reverse, keeping perfect backwards time.

Of course, had anyone started to inquire about it, I would have pled the Fifth.

After Grandma passed, the clock quietly went to an aunt's house, and no one was the wiser — the key conveniently lost, of course.

Of course, the clock wasn't my only experiment.

Somewhere between childhood curiosity and sheer mischief, I decided to build a volcano — and not a tiny tabletop one, either. It was actually for the school science fair. I still remember it like it was yesterday.

It was a two-foot by two-foot monster, balanced precariously on a piece of half-inch plywood, shaped entirely by me. I started with chicken wire to form the mountain, then layered on a homemade adobe mixture to sculpt the cone. To make it look alive, I tumbled sawdust in green food coloring and glued it to the slopes as foliage.

By the time I was done, it was heavy as me, proud as anything I'd ever made, and smelled faintly of wet clay and sawdust — like the outdoors trapped in my garage.

The recipe for the lava provided by school was lame — just vinegar, baking soda, and a little red food coloring. I, of course, had to "improve" on it.

I combined the powder from some old fireworks with the phosphorus from a pack of matches crammed into the base of the volcano's cone. It was strictly scientific, I told myself.

Absolutely controlled. Totally safe… mostly.

On the day of the fair, the volcano was an eye-catcher. I'd gotten permission to use a match to light it — concerns everywhere, of course — but after I vehemently promised it would just release smoke, the teachers relented.

I struck the match.

At first, it worked perfectly. Smoke curled lazily out of the top; the judges smiled and congratulated me on my "excellent engineering and creativity." I was beaming. First place was mine for sure.

And then everything went sideways. What started as a gentle puff of smoke quickly escalated into hissing, sparks shooting out the top of the cone like a miniature fireworks show.

The red food coloring and salt in my mixture melted into molten-like lava that oozed down the sides, slipping into the cracks I'd sculpted earlier.

Why salt and food coloring? I honestly don't remember — maybe it was just a filler, maybe I thought it would make the lava "pop."

Either way, it worked.

The heat made the plywood smell like scorched toast, and the tang of phosphorus stung my nose. My masterpiece had turned into a small, writhing inferno, and for a moment, I wasn't sure whether to cheer or run.

"Whoa! Did his volcano just sneeze fire?" a classmate shouted.

"I think it's… alive!" another whispered, ducking behind a table.

The principal did not see it that way.

“Mariano Velez!” he barked, emerging from a plume of smoke, fists balled and planted firmly on his hips. “What in heaven’s name do you think you’re doing? This is school, not a pyrotechnics competition!”

“I-I just… wanted it to look real,” I stammered, stepping back as a trickle of lava hissed past my sneakers.

“Real? Do you know how many fire extinguishers nearly got used today? How many smoke alarms you set off?!” He wagged a finger like a missile locked on target. “This is serious, young man. You are lucky no one was hurt!”

I nodded furiously, cheeks flaming, as sparks continued to spit out of the cone. Somewhere in the back, the judges awkwardly clapped, probably unsure whether to congratulate me or call the fire department. My first-place dreams evaporated faster than the smoke curling from my masterpiece.

That evening, Dad couldn’t resist telling the story at our weekly carne asada. My uncles were doubled over in laughter, wiping tears from their eyes.

“So let me get this straight,” my Uncle Frank gasped between chuckles, “your science project almost burned down the school… and you thought it was okay?”

Dad leaned back, taking a slow sip of his beer. “Well, it was a volcano, and almost a disaster. But it got people talking. And it looked great… for a few minutes, anyway. Kid’s creative, I’ll give him that.”

I joined in the laughter, my embarrassment softening into pride. Sure, I hadn’t walked away with a ribbon, but I had built something unforgettable — a volcano that, for a few glorious seconds, truly came alive, complete with fire, smoke, and molten red lava.

And in that moment, I realized some victories are measured in sparks and awe, not medals.

Over time, tinkering turned into fixing. Both my brother and I became regular shop assistants for Dad. Remodeling projects weren't just chores — they were opportunities to hone our abilities and help keep costs down. We learned everything from drywalling to running electrical wire, from basic vehicle maintenance to carpentry.

My first real feat of at-home, real-world engineering happened the day I "borrowed" my mom's car for a joyride. I was fifteen, flying down the street in the '76 Mercury Cougar, windows down, wind in my hair — pure outlaw freedom. That lasted right up until a sharp, fast turn made the engine sputter and die, smoke curling out from under the hood.

PANIC.

I wrestled the Cougar to the curb on what little momentum it had left (no power steering is cruel on skinny teenage arms), then popped the hood. Sparks sizzled against the metal, and the faint smell of ozone made my nose twitch.

The battery had tipped sideways, and the positive terminal had welded itself to the body, frying the ground cable beyond recognition.

I slammed the hood, leaned into the bumper, and pushed — inch by sweaty inch — all the way to the driveway. My arms burned, my back ached, and the smell of hot rubber from the tires sticking to the asphalt made me gag.

Once in the driveway, I raided the tool shed for wrenches, pulled the battery, and hooked it to the charger. I remembered a stash of cables my dad kept for "someday," found one close enough to the dead ground strap, and cut it to length. Terminals, though — I needed new ones.

I grabbed five bucks, biked to the auto-parts store, and fifteen minutes later — $2.49 poorer — I was back installing my first custom ground cable.

"Be careful, kid," my brother called from the garage doorway, eyeing the sparks popping whenever I touched a wrench to the battery. "This thing's gonna eat your fingers!"

I ignored him, tightened the bolts, re-seated the battery, and climbed behind the wheel. Moment of truth: I turned the key and… vrooooom! The Cougar roared back to life, shaking as though it had been napping and just woken up cranky. Victory was mine.

My dad never seemed the wiser (or maybe he noticed and chose not to say a word). Years later, at one of our carne asadas, I finally confessed. He just smiled, nodded, and took a slow sip of his beer — the kind of look that said, *I knew all along, but you needed the lesson more than the scolding.*

My Dad was the biggest tinkerer of them all. He was always working on something — around the house, in the garage, on the cars — his hands never idle, his mind always turning over some new problem to solve or project to start.

Watching him was like seeing creativity and practicality collide, and we couldn't help but follow along, picking up tricks, shortcuts, and little hacks that would stick with us for life.

These days, I tinker simply because it makes me happy. Old cameras, stubborn lawnmowers, the occasional wobbly chair — all fair game.

With Google and AI at my fingertips, I could probably talk myself through minor surgery… though I'm smart enough to leave my own insides alone.

Still, every time I coax some cranky appliance back to life, I feel like that kid again — part detective, part magician, and entirely certain that whatever I'm "fixing" wasn't really broken until I started helping.

There's a thrill in taking something ordinary, something discarded or stubborn, and breathing life back into it. A creak becomes a click, a spark becomes a hum, and suddenly, the impossible feels possible.

Sometimes I think of that little clock, running backwards somewhere in the house of memory, and the volcano that erupted like fireworks in a school gym.

They remind me that tinkering isn't just about fixing or building; it's about curiosity, courage, and joy. I

t's about daring to poke, pry, and play, and discovering in the process that you can shape the world — even just a little — with your own two hands.

And if I'm lucky, someone like my dad is watching, smiling over a beer, knowing that the spirit of invention lives on.

UNDER THE HOOD:

LESSONS FROM A FIRST CAR

Under the Hood: Lessons from a First Car

There is something undeniably special about one's first car. It doesn't matter if it was a hand-me-down, a clunker that coughed itself awake every morning, or a gleaming machine you washed every Saturday like it was a sacred ritual—your first car wasn't just transportation.

It was freedom on four wheels. It was the key to every late-night adventure you shouldn't have been on, every early-morning drive to a job you didn't really want, every mixtape-fueled cruise through the streets of your hometown, windows down, pretending you were the main character in a movie.

A first car was a classroom too, teaching lessons no adult bothered to explain.

Like how to coax a stubborn engine into starting when it was 112 degrees and raining outside.

How to pray with sincerity when the gas light flickered on ten miles from home.

How to roll down a window that had long ago given up its will to live.

And how to strike that delicate balance between pride and embarrassment when you pulled up somewhere important and hoped it wouldn't stall in front of everyone.

But more than anything, a first car was a little pocket of independence—a tiny metal world that belonged only to you.

The glove compartment held your secrets, the backseat your messes, the dashboard your dreams of everywhere you might someday go.

For me, that freedom came wrapped in root-beer brown metal. My first car was a '76 Mercury Cougar XR7—root-beer brown with a tan interior, the kind of color combo that made it look like a rolling Werther's Original.

Under that long hood sat a 351-2V V8 (5.8L) engine with a four-barrel carburetor and a 3-speed SelectShift automatic transmission. More than enough power for a 17-year-old to feel unstoppable… and also more than enough to get me into trouble, which it absolutely did (even though I had no idea what any of those things meant).

Honestly, back then I thought "351-2V" meant it had two volts. Two! As in, one step above a double-A battery. I just repeated it because it sounded cool.

Adults would ask, "What's under the hood?"

And I'd puff my chest out and answer, "A 351-2V V8."

They'd nod respectfully, and I'd nod back like I actually understood what they were nodding about.

It wasn't until months later—after a guy at the auto parts store laughed in my face—that I realized it had nothing to do with volts and everything to do with "venturi," which, in my 17-year-old brain, sounded like either an Italian wine or a character from Star Trek.

But ignorance never stopped me from believing that Mercury could outrun practically anything in Calexico: Chevys, Fords, wind gusts, chihuahuas—didn't matter.

Put me behind that oversized steering wheel, with the hood stretching out like the deck of an aircraft carrier, and suddenly I was Maverick from Top Gun… just driving three blocks to school. And stopping twice because I forgot my backpack.

Back then, fuel was $0.88 a gallon. Three bucks could keep me cruising for a week—granted, my "cruising" consisted mostly of driving three blocks to school and back, pretending the Cougar needed to downshift dramatically to make the turn into the student parking lot.

That Cougar made me feel like I was somebody—like an adult, or at least the idea of an adult. It was loud, proud, expensive to fill at a time when I barely had lunch money, and it shook every time it idled like it was trying to cough up a secret.

But it was mine. And for a 17-year-old kid in the 80s, that alone was magic.

Like any kid with his first set of wheels, I treated that car better than I treated myself. It got washed once a week and polished daily with a terrycloth rag that lived permanently in the backseat.

I remember one afternoon washing it out in front of the house, the sun beating down, the smell of soap and wet concrete in the air. My dad was doing handyman stuff, my nephew Junior was running around being Junior, and I was finishing up—hosing down the driveway, putting away the bucket, admiring my reflection in the paint.

Then I heard it: giggling.

I turned slowly.

"NNNOOOOOOOOOOOOO!!!"

There was Junior, beaming with pride, holding the hose full blast and "helping" by rinsing the car again… starting from scratch. Water streaks everywhere. Soap running down the sides.

My dad? Doubled over, laughing one of those deep, seismic belly laughs.

"¡Ándale, mijo! A empezar de nuevo," he said between laughs.

"Pero esta vez… con ayudante."

More laughter.

My mom stepped outside to see what the noise was about, took one look, and covered her mouth—trying not to let the giggle escape.

I wanted to laugh, too.

I also wanted to cry.

Mostly I just stood there, soaked, defeated, and suddenly very aware that toddlers with hoses are a force of nature.

But that car was more than just transportation—it was where I learned things.

It was on that Cougar that I discovered the joy—and occasional terror—of mechanical upgrades. My dad didn't call it "upgrading," though. He called it "metiendo mano donde no debes."

The first project was simple: spark-plug wires and a new distributor. At least, that's what the instructions made it sound like.

I had the hood open, wires everywhere, arms covered in grease up to the elbows. My dad walked by, hammer in hand, wiping sweat from his forehead.

"¿Qué estás haciendo ahora?" he asked.

"Upgrading," I replied confidently.

He stared at the engine. Then at me.

"¿Cómo sabes cuál cable va dónde?"

I shrugged. "I… marked most of them."

"Most." He set the hammer down. "Ay Dios mío."

But somehow, hours later, after a few accidental sparks ("That wasn't me—that was the wrench!") and my dad crossing himself twice, the Cougar rumbled to life. A little rough at first, like it had swallowed a gravel shake, but once it smoothed out, I felt like an automotive surgeon.

Once one project worked, I got bold.

Next came the carburetor upgrade—the four-barrel I was convinced would turn the Cougar into a drag-strip legend. I remember laying out all the parts on an old beach towel like a surgeon prepping for a transplant.

My dad peeked over my shoulder.

"Mijo… why are there extra screws in that pile?"

"They're… optional."

"Optional?"

"Yeah," I said, tapping the carb gently with a screwdriver.

"After-market weight reduction."

He didn't laugh. But my nephew Junior did, probably because he didn't know what we were talking about.

Installing the larger radiator was a whole other adventure. I'd read somewhere—probably a photocopied magazine page folded in my wallet—that a bigger radiator would keep the Cougar cooler, especially in the Calexico heat.

What the instructions didn't mention was that the radiator weighed approximately 600 pounds and had the personality of a stubborn mule. (Well, not really, but it felt like it).

I was in the driveway wrestling it like I was trying to pin it for a WWE championship. My mom came outside, saw me red-faced and sweating, and asked:

"¿Quieres agua?"

"No, I'm good," I grunted, straining.

"Mijo, you're about to pass out."

She had a point.

Eventually Dad came out to help, which really meant he held it steady while I tried to bolt it in without dropping it on my foot.

The moment we finished, he stepped back and nodded.

"Looks good," he said.

"Yeah," I replied proudly. "It'll run cooler now."

He looked at the Cougar, then back at me.

"Or explode," he added, with a smile.

Then he went back inside like he hadn't just cursed the project.

But the crown jewel—the upgrade that made the Cougar mine—was the sound system.

It started with the Pioneer pull-out cassette deck. The moment I slid it into place and felt that click, I swear angels sang. Then came the equalizer—the kind with the dancing LED lights that made the dashboard look like a mini Vegas strip.

My dad watched me wiring it all together, cables everywhere.

“Why does the radio need so many wires?” he asked.

“Because it has… features.”

He raised an eyebrow. “Like what? NASA?”

Then came the 12-inch speakers I salvaged from my dad’s old radio console, which was probably from the Nixon era. He was ready to throw it out.

“Wait! I need those speakers!”

“¿Para qué? They don’t even sound good anymore.”

“That’s because they’re old,” I said. “But in a box, powered right, they’ll thump.”

He just stared at me like I was speaking Martian.

Building the speaker box in the garage was a whole weekend project. Sawdust everywhere. Measurements that almost lined up. My dad poked his head in once and said:

“That box is crooked. Esta chueca!”

“No,” I lied. “It’s… acoustically designed.”

“It’s crooked.”

He wasn’t wrong. But it fit in the trunk, and when I finally wired everything up and hit play—BOOM. The rearview mirror buzzed. The trunk latch rattled. My mom came outside thinking something had exploded.

“¡Ay! ¿Qué fue eso?”

“Music,” I shouted.

“That’s not music—that’s an earthquake!”

I grinned. Perfect.

Those upgrades made the Cougar louder, faster, cooler—okay, maybe not faster, but definitely more dramatic. But more than anything, they turned that car into my classroom, my workshop, my pride and joy. Every bolt, every spark, every accidental electrocution—worth it.

This was my baby.

I remember my dad telling me about his first car—a 1953 Pontiac Chieftain 2-door Hardtop Coupé. Black. Sleek. Mean. Just hearing about it made you sit up straighter. He admitted he was a greenhorn when it came to cars, and this one in particular was a lot for a young man's first ride.

He saved every penny he could, working until he had enough to cover the $300 price tag—about $2,667 in 2025 dollars.

He'd say that back in his day, owning one wasn't just transportation, it was a rite of passage. A measuring stick. A badge of honor. He talked about it the way some people talk about their first love: eyes half-squinted, smiling like he was replaying an old home movie only he could see.

He laughed when he told me that, shaking his head like he could still feel the weight of that hood and the responsibility that came with it. "Demasiado carro para un chamaco," he'd say. Too much car for a kid. But it was also the only way he learned—by diving straight into the deep end with something that growled louder than he did.

He told me how the Chieftain had quirks, real personality. How the engine wouldn't start unless you pumped the gas just right. How the choke stuck when it was cold, how the steering wheel felt like trying to turn a cement mixer, and how the brakes had what he called "a suggestion mode"—they only worked when they felt like it.

"But I loved that carro," he'd say, tapping his chest. "It taught me everything."

And that's when he'd shift from nostalgia to advice mode—the Dad Gear. He'd tell me about learning to change his oil in the dirt driveway, about swapping spark plugs by trial and error, about burning his fingers more times than he could count. He talked about listening to the engine like it was speaking a language only time and frustration could teach you.

"You don't learn with perfect cars," he'd say. "You learn with the ones that fight back."

And he said it with pride, like every scraped knuckle he ever earned under that hood made him who he was.

What I didn't realize then—standing there with grease on my hands, halfway through another questionable "upgrade" on the Cougar—was that he wasn't just telling me about his Chieftain. He was telling me about becoming a man.

He'd say, "Mijo, cuando tienes tu primer carro… ya eres hombre."

And then he'd add, "Pero sólo si lo puedes arreglar."

And years later, when my own car fought me back, I finally understood.

A car fights you.
A car teaches you.
A car makes you earn every mile.

To him, and to a whole generation before mine, having a car wasn't enough. You had to know it—inside, outside, underneath. You had to change your own oil, gap your own spark plugs, tighten your own belts, and hit the starter with a hammer in just the right spot when it refused to cooperate. He made it sound like your relationship with your car was half romance, half wrestling match.

"There's an art to how you maintain your ride," he'd say, wiping his hands on an old T-shirt that used to be white sometime in the Nixon era. "Anybody can own a car. A man takes care of his."

I think about that a lot now—especially when I see kids driving around in these sleek, whisper-quiet spaceships with more computer chips than personality. Cars that practically apologize if you drift out of your lane. Cars that beep, buzz, warn, guide, brake, park, and probably give relationship advice if you dig far enough into the menu.

These kids? They've never opened a hood unless it's to take a photo for social media. They don't know the smell of hot oil or the sound of a loose timing chain. They don't know the heartbreak of dropping a bolt into the engine bay and hearing it ping-ping-ping into a place you will never, ever be able to reach again. They don't know what it's like to climb under a car on a hot summer day and stand up so covered in grease that your mom makes you change outside.

Nowadays if something breaks, they plug it into a computer. Back then, you plugged yourself into the car—sometimes literally, via static shock.

Sometimes I wonder if we had it better. Not better cars—no, today's engines could run on hopes and dreams and still make it to Yuma and back without a hiccup. But better stories. Better memories. Better bruised knuckles.

There was pride in saying, "Yeah, I fixed that."

Even if the "fix" involved duct tape, a borrowed part from a neighbor's junk pile, and the grace of God.

That's what my dad taught me. That's what the Cougar taught me. A car wasn't just something you used—it was something you learned, something you cared for, something that taught you patience, persistence, and which cuss words you shouldn't say around your mother.

And in that way, owning that beast of a Mercury didn't just make me feel like a man.

It made me feel like my father's son.

And what was all this tinkering with the car for?

To show off, of course.

Cruising was the goal. We all talked about it. It was what we were gonna do Friday after the football game.

Well, we didn't exactly go cruising.

Most of the time, the Cougar's long hood and rumbling V8 got me from school to home, or maybe to the corner store for whatever my mom had scribbled on the grocery list.

But every trip was a performance, whether anyone else knew it or not.

Every stoplight was a chance to look cool. Foot hovering over the gas, windows down, music just loud enough to make heads turn.

Pulling into the gas station was practically a spectator sport: you never missed a chance to rev the engine when friends were around, let that V8 growl, let the lights flash off the paint, let everyone know the Cougar had arrived.

Even the smallest errands became excuses for drama. Stopping at the store? Might as well make it a runway. Rolling into the driveway with groceries in the trunk? Extra points if you could rev the engine and pretend you'd been in a street race on the way home—even if the only race was against the clock to get back before Mom realized you'd taken the long way.

It wasn't about speed. It was about presence. About attitude. About turning a three-block commute into an event. And every time I climbed behind that wheel, I felt like I owned the street—

even if the street was just a stretch of cracked asphalt between the high school and the grocery store.

The Cougar didn't just take me places.

It gave me a voice.

A swagger.

And a small, very teen-aged taste of freedom.

Ribs, Paint, Plastic Heroes ...and Us

Ribs, Paint, Plastic Heroes ...and Us

I didn't fully understand it back then, not really. I just knew that my parents were always moving—always doing something, always busy. My dad worked for the city's Street Department, the crew everyone seemed to know but no one thought much about.

They handled everything: patching streets, maintaining the iconic palms along the city's streets, keeping the parks clean and green, making sure the city didn't fall apart.

Visits to his workplace were rare, but we often saw him on duty when running errands with my mom, or mowing the grass in the park next to school. He'd always make sure to be on the playground side during recess, and I'd run out there, heart racing, just to catch a glimpse.

The moment our eyes met, I'd light up—waving as hard as I could—and he'd stop, wave back, and flash that quiet smile that somehow made the whole day feel brighter.

And my mom... well, she handled everything else.

Every night, she orchestrated the chaos of our home like it was her job—because it was. From the laundry to the meals, the homework, the arguments, the little emergencies that popped up at all hours. She was always on call, her energy quiet but unending. We didn't notice it at the time, not really. We didn't realize that every meal she made, every shelf she straightened, every gentle reprimand, was her way of keeping the family together, of making life work, even when it was hard.

Looking back now, I can feel it—the weight of their work, the way they carried it all silently so that we could run through our childhood without a hitch. I didn't know to call it sacrifice then. I didn't even know the word "dedication" had a face.

But I could feel it, in the rhythm of our days, in the steady heartbeat of our house, in the safety of knowing that no matter what, someone was holding it all together.

It's funny how you only realize the depth of these things when you're older—how your parents' efforts, invisible at the time, become the backbone of all your memories. The streets my dad patched, the meals my mom cooked, the laundry folded neatly in drawers—they were more than chores or jobs.

They were proof that love often looks like work, and that the quiet, everyday acts of care are the ones that build a life worth remembering.

Those memories threaded themselves through the small, ordinary places we spent our days—the corner stores, the playgrounds, the parks—each one carrying its own distinct rhythm of sights, sounds, and smells.

I don't remember the exact year FedMart closed, but I remember the years it stayed alive. They live in my mind in permanent neon: the tang of rubbery floor polish mixing with the faint metallic scent of automotive aisles, the polished tile that always felt slightly sticky under your sneakers, and the distant clang of someone dropping a wrench near the back.

FedMart wasn't just a store—it was part of a little revolution. Back in the day, it was called the original "superstore." Bigger than a grocery store, bigger than a hardware shop, it was this strange, ambitious mash-up of everything you could need under one roof: food, clothes, toys, paint, appliances, electronics. It felt like someone had tried to build an entire town inside a building and mostly succeeded. You could get a gallon of paint, a box of cereal, and a toy all in one trip, and somehow the aisles made sense, even if your brain begged to disagree. It even had its own gas station and auto shop. It was truly an all-in-one place.

And Dad—always Dad—walking fast, keys jingling, name tag slightly crooked, heading toward the paint department like a man reporting for duty on a ship he secretly loved. He worked a regular day job, the kind that left dust in the folds of his sleeves and a low hum of fatigue in his eyes, the kind of tired adults carry without anyone telling them how heavy it is.

Then, after a quick dinner and a coffee so strong it could sand a deck, he'd head out again to FedMart.

Said he liked the work.
Said the extra money helped.
Said it gave him something to do.

But now, looking back, I think he liked belonging somewhere. Somewhere bright, somewhere warm, somewhere he knew exactly where every drop cloth, paint scraper, and gallon of semi-gloss lived.

He made a difference.

To me, though? FedMart wasn't a job. FedMart was magic.

The magic started with the ribs. Always the ribs.

FedMart's café sat off to the right of the entrance, tucked off to the side (but in front of the long row of registers), but you could smell it before you saw it. It wasn't big—half a dozen tables, a counter, a cooler humming like it had asthma—but it served the greatest BBQ ribs ever created by human hands. The smoke curled into the air and clung to your clothes like a memory. If heaven had a smokehouse, it smelled like that place.

We'd visit Dad on some evenings, Mom guiding us past displays of laundry baskets and discount towels, the three of us making a beeline for the café. She'd hold our hands as we stepped over sticky floors, murmuring little jokes to keep our patience intact, occasionally giving the cashier a wink when he scowled. Mom had a way of smoothing the rough edges of everything—even a grocery store cafeteria.

The guy behind the counter always looked like he moonlighted as a bounty hunter. His apron had stains older than I was, and the clang of utensils on trays rang like a small percussion orchestra behind the counter. But he made ribs so tender they practically confessed their sins when you picked them up. The sauce stuck to your fingers, sweet and smoky, leaving sticky fingerprints on the Styrofoam tray.

We'd sit under buzzing fluorescent lights, the intercom hovering above us like a polite ghost: "Attention FedMart shoppers, the sporting goods department will be closing in ten minutes." The voice always sounded bored. Or tired. Or like it had personally given up on sporting goods.

Meanwhile, we'd peel ribs off bones with our fingers, faces smeared with sauce, Mom wiping our cheeks with a napkin dipped in her iced tea because she said it worked better than water. It didn't. But it smelled nice, a mix of tangy smoke and sugar that lingered in your nostrils long after the first bite.

When we finished, Mom would usher us through aisles to find Dad. I remember stepping from the polished floors into the cooler, grittier vibe of hardware, where the smell of plywood mixed with paint thinner in a way that somehow felt… safe.

Dad belonged there the way birds belong to trees. Sometimes he brought the ribs home; they made for some excellent leftover meals the next day. Mom, meanwhile, kept an eye on the floor displays, nudged stray cans back into place, and quietly kept the store from becoming a mess as we tore through it.

Sometimes, after his shift, Dad would bring home a cardboard box. Nothing fancy. Just a big, flattened-out FedMart box stuffed with the toys that had been returned, opened, or broken. He'd tuck it in the corner of the living room and leave it there, and then we'd go to bed, knowing something awaited us in the morning.

Saturday mornings were the best. We'd wake up, still groggy, sunlight spilling through the curtains, the smell of coffee, eggs, and tortillas drifting in from the kitchen. And then we'd see it—the box. It called to us. We'd leap in like kids diving into a pile of leaves, the cardboard edges scratching our arms, the toys tumbling around us, their small plastic voices and squeaks filling the air.

Stretch Armstrong was there, once missing an arm, once missing an eyebrow, always missing dignity. We stretched him across the front yard once—farther than any toy was meant to endure (I want to say it must have been ten yards easy). He resisted. He groaned, or maybe that was us.

Then, with a soft thup like a grape exploding, his arm split and this cold, oozy, corn-syrup-looking alien goo dribbled out. We screamed like witnesses to a war crime. Dad came in, saw the scene, sighed, and said, "Well… he stretched." And went back to reading the paper.

The Six Million Dollar Man had a cracked bionic eye, which made everything look like the world was melting slightly to the left. Did it matter? No. He still ran in slow motion better than any of us ever could. My brother and I fought wars for this one—or so we thought—but like brothers always do, we ended up sharing.

Our Tonka trucks were already indestructible, but the FedMart versions had special dents that told stories.

Lite-Brite boxes were always missing half the pegs but still magical.

Simon's red button worked only if you punched it with the force of a thousand suns, but we played anyway. Hot Wheels had missing wheels, missing windows, missing everything but a chassis—and still they were perfect.

Looking back, none of the toys were whole. But somehow they were enough. Maybe because we were whole when we played with them.

As a kid, you don't think about what a second job means. You don't think about clocking out at one job only to clock in at another. You just think: Dad works at FedMart.

Dad knows everything.

Dad brings the box home.

And Mom… Mom made sure the journey there and back felt like magic.

Sometimes I'd catch Dad leaning on a counter, rubbing his eyes, drinking cold coffee from a Styrofoam cup, the bitter liquid lingering on his tongue. And Mom, quietly corralling us through aisles, carrying patience like a shield, kept it all together. As I grew older, the picture sharpened: they weren't there just for paint or toys. They were there for us.

Sometimes we'd leave the store late, the kind of late where the parking lot lights hummed and moths held their own midnight convention around them. Dad would walk us to the car, carrying his lunch pail, the scent of paint and ribs clinging to him like cologne.

Mom would give him that sideways glance that said thank you without words. Backseat full of half-broken toys, hands still sticky from dinner. The ride home was quiet, but it hummed with love.

Looking out the window, watching the lights drift by, I always felt like FedMart wasn't just a store. It was a chapter. A warm, bright, slightly chaotic chapter full of ribs, toys, and tired parents doing their best.

And now, all these years later, I realize something: Dad didn't just run the paint department.

Mom didn't just run the home.

They ran the nights and days. They ran the effort.

They ran the quiet sacrifices that built our world—one shift, one aisle, one box of discarded toys at a time.

FedMart is long gone now.

Dad has been retired for many years.

Mom's been gone a little over a year now.

And me? I'm still reliving those memories, still putting the countless lessons they taught me to use.

But those Saturday mornings… those visits with Mom and Dad at the store… the smell of smoke and paint, the sticky fingers, the chaos, the quiet love—they are forever.

Even now, they feel alive, tucked in the corners of my heart, a chapter that will never close.

the Flavor of Family

The Flavor of Family

Food has a way of doing what nothing else can: it gathers us, roots us, and reminds us who we are. In our family, meals were never just about eating. They were the soundtrack of our childhood—the punctuation marks on our days—the reason the house smelled like love, garlic, cumin, and chaos all at once.

From the sizzle of papas fritas in the morning to the smoky aroma of carne asada drifting through the backyard, every dish carried a memory. Every bite was a story waiting to be told.

Kitchens became stages, dining rooms became arenas, and backyards turned into dusty playgrounds of laughter, shouting, last-minute arguments, and the occasional minor disaster that everyone remembered slightly differently. A tortilla flips onto the floor and someone picks it up anyway; my brother sneakily grabs a piece of papas fritas before anyone sees.

Family and food were inseparable. You couldn't pull them apart any more than you could pull beans out of rice. Every gathering—whether a midweek meal, a "quick" cookout that somehow grew legs, or a holiday feast—was a celebration of us simply being us. The flavors, the smells, the spills, the shouting, the laughter—they all blended into a messy, glorious symphony of togetherness.

In our house, the table wasn't just a place to eat. It was a stage for connection, a hub for bonding, a battleground for debates over whose flauta was actually the best (for the record: everyone knew, but we pretended it was a mystery). It was a canvas for stories that painted themselves into memory, splattered with salsa stains and the occasional fork mark. Decades later, you could still close your eyes and taste them.

Caldo de res bubbled on chilly days… and also on those 95-degree Imperial Valley afternoons when turning on the stove should've been illegal.

Menudo on Sundays demanded bravery from anyone bold enough to peek into the pot—especially if you weren't sure whether Mom had added extra pata that day.

Steam rising, nose hairs singed, spicy aroma punching the back of your throat.

YUMMOS!!! (as my brother would often say at the table).

And the salsa de molcajete? It didn't just wake up your taste buds—no, hombre.

It punched them in the throat, slapped them on the back, and asked what they were gonna do about it.

"¡Ma! ¡Está picosa la salsa?"

"No creo, mijo. A mí no se me hizo picosa," she'd say, stirring the pot like she hadn't just weaponized chiles in our own home.

But we all knew better.

If she said it was mild, that meant it was hot.

If she thought it was spicy, it was going to melt your teeth, cauterize your sinuses, and kill your taste buds for a good three days.

The mornings when there was nothing else to do—no chores, no errands, no responsibilities—were the best kind. The house smelled like possibilities, and the kitchen smelled like love… and fire.

On the stove, homemade tortillas curled at the edges, golden and warm, pockets of steam popping up, waiting to catch the first scoop of frijolitos.

The eggs were huevos estrellados, sunny and runny, spilling over the beans like molten gold. Papas fritas—tiny pops of oil that sounded like applause.

Fresh salsa tatemada sat in a little bowl, smoky and tangy, daring you to dip, drizzle, or pour without guilt.

We'd sit at the table, shoulders brushing, spoons clinking against bowls, the steam rising and curling around us, filling the room with warmth. And the cafecito con leche—rich, sweet, strong—was the final

touch, a little cup of liquid comfort that made everything taste like childhood.

No rush. No plans. Just the quiet joy of good food, shared company, and the kind of mornings that felt like they could last forever.

On school days, while other kids stayed at school for lunch—trading sandwiches for a cold bowl of chili with semi-stale cornbread, or sipping from tiny milk cartons—we had a different plan. My brother and I would walk the familiar route home, backpacks bouncing, shoes kicking up dust, stomachs rumbling in anticipation.

Backpacks were dropped mid-step because Mom was already in the kitchen, whistling like a mariachi solo gone rogue, flipping tortillas with the confidence of someone who'd done it ten thousand times. She laid out plates like she was staging a

Broadway musical—big flour tortillas for everyone except the one cousin who swore they tasted different from brand to brand.

The smell hit us first, before we even stepped through the door: pollo frito drifting down the block like a scent-based invitation. Mom was making fried chicken again.

It was gonna be lit.

That also meant pepinitos con limón, and sopita de arroz simmering in the pot, sending little waves of comfort through the kitchen air.

Other days, it was tacos dorados, crisp and golden, lined up like soldiers on a plate. Or enchiladas, soft and warm, drenched in rich, homemade salsa, beckoning from the table. And on the side, a steaming bowl of sopita de fideo, comforting and simple, its aroma promising warmth and nourishment.

The air in the kitchen was always a little thick with the scent of frying, simmering, and tortillas fresh off the comal. Plates clattered, spoons clinked, and napkins were inevitably stolen from each other mid-reach.

Every bite was a tiny victory, every sip of agua fresca or lightly sweetened milk a reminder that home was better than any cafeteria could ever be.

Lunch wasn't just about eating—it was about walking in from the world outside, shedding the classroom noise, and diving into a little pocket of perfection.

Then came the cookouts. Ah, the carnes asadas.

Picture this: Tíos wielding tongs like they'd trained for this moment their whole lives, arguing over grill space and whether the meat needed more salt or "love" (same thing, apparently).

Tías orchestrating a side-dish assembly line worthy of NASA—potato salad, nopales, pico, beans that had been simmering since the Pleistocene era.

Cousins darted around like caffeinated bandits—one minute scaling a tree as if auditioning for a circus, the next tumbling through the dirt like some kind of feral pack.

They made regular "hit-and-run" raids on the grill, snatching a piece of carne asada here, a hot tortilla there, disappearing before anyone could say a word.

Every so often, you'd catch a flash of laughter or a cloud of dust and just shake your head. There was no real strategy, no rules, only chaos, speed, and the unspoken code that whatever landed on your plate first… well, it was yours.

Dogs barking in harmony, hoping someone—anyone—would drop a piece of carne.

Carne asada is a tradition anywhere Mexican culture thrives—but if you grew up splitting time between Calexico and Mexicali, it takes on a mythic quality.

It becomes the heartbeat of family life. A seasonal ritual. A smoky, sizzling anthem. A rhythm so familiar it lived in your bones.

Growing up, carnes asadas weren't just meals—they were full-scale, multi-generational productions. And I'm not talking, "let's grill a few things and call it a day."

No, Chale.

These events were legendary. They started as casual visits—"just stopping by"—and somehow transformed into full-blown reunions celebrating absolutely nothing except the holy miracle that everyone was there.

Stories erupted over the sizzle of meat. Songs broke out spontaneously, usually when someone found the old Vicente Fernandez CD. One cookout often turned into the planning meeting for the next—like some chaotic, unofficial board meeting of Family, Inc.

As we got older, the chaos shifted. We claimed our roles:

I became the Grill Master, wielding tongs like Excalibur.

My sisters rotated between side dishes and slicing meat with surgical precision.

My brother contributed by asking, "Do we have more meat?" every five minutes—an important job, if you ask him.

Mom and Dad reclined like monarchs, cold drinks in hand, letting us run the circus they had spent decades perfecting.

And still—still—the magic never faded.

An uncle would arrive unannounced. Someone would sprint to buy more tortillas because we always underestimated ourselves. Cousins would reappear with grass stains, mystery bruises, and absolutely no explanation.

And somehow the cookout would grow louder, bigger, warmer—immeasurably better.

It wasn't just a meal. It was theater, comedy, opera, and tradition all rolled into one smoky, greasy, love-soaked afternoon.

There was one cookout, though, that lives in my memory like it was staged by angels with questionable judgment. It was two parts family gathering, ten parts potluck. It began with a simple idea—"No carne asada this time."

It was blasphemous.

It was treasonous.

But somehow, it worked.

We stumbled into our first (and possibly last) full-blown family fry-out. The spread was ridiculous: tacos dorados, flautas, tostadas, sopes, even some deep-fried ribs—greasy, glorious, unapologetically over-the-top. I don't remember who suggested it. I don't know what triggered it.

All I know is that once the first pot of oil heated up, the family transformed into a fry brigade, and nothing was safe.

Every bite felt like a tiny celebration. Every plate was a sculpture of golden, crispy excess. Laughter bounced off walls like we were trying to crack the tiles. Cousins zoomed around like sugar-addicted squirrels. Adults debated—loudly and lovingly—over whose taco was the best. It was pure, chaotic, delicious togetherness.

By the end of the night, after a few too many beers, karaoke took over. Well… if I'm being honest, it wasn't really karaoke so much as us belting out Juan Gabriel songs at the top of our lungs. We had no autotune, most of us were hopelessly off-key, and yet no one cared. It was a chorus of family, of love, of life—messy, loud, and utterly unforgettable.

It reminded us why we loved just being us.

But it wasn't just the cookouts. Oh no. The cook-ins were their own spectacle—indoor feasts that turned kitchens into aromatic combat zones.

Holiday seasons meant tamales stacked like construction material, buñuelos dusted in sugar drifts, pots of menudo or pozole simmering away like they had something to prove, potato salad chilling in the fridge like a backstage diva, sopita de arroz calming even the crankiest souls.

These meals were comfort food for the most uncomfortably comfortable family imaginable.

Everyone had a role—or at least an opinion—about what belonged on the table. Someone inevitably dropped a tortilla. Someone else spilled salsa like it was part of the décor. And someone always yelled, "Did anyone bother to bring ice?"—as if the cookout could not possibly continue without it.

Kids ran between rooms like miniature hurricanes, their energy undampened by the clatter of pots, the occasional scream from a man losing his mind over the baseball game on TV, or the ladies chismiando in the back room, exchanging gossip like it was currency.

It was a symphony of chaos—every sound and movement perfectly timed, perfectly imperfect. And somehow, amidst the spilled salsa, the kids darting through the air like tiny comets, and the endless laughter, it all worked.

As the liquid libations entered our systems, the stories inevitably took over the night. Someone would pass the tongs, someone else would crack open a fresh beer, and suddenly the conversation shifted from bills and work schedules to the legendary adventures of our youth—told, of course, with humorous embellishment, exaggerated bravado, and the kind of creative liberties only carne asada smoke can inspire.

And always—always—a good time.

Turns out this was also how our parents learned about the inexplicable incidents of our childhood and adolescent years. (I guess if you're gonna confess, there's no better way to do it than with a beer in one hand and a taco in the other.)

Like how beers kept vanishing from the fridge or mysteriously showing up open and half empty. My brother and I would sneak a drink here and there… until the day we were caught in the back room, sitting on the couch and singing our little hearts out—me with one arm draped around my brother, and him holding the beer between us like it was the microphone in our impromptu duet.

Or how we took generous sips of Mom's "grape juice," the one that always made me feel a little "funny." (Turns out it wasn't grape juice at all—it was her stash of wine. Who knew Concord could kick like that?)

Yeah… this is also how Mom and Dad finally found out what really happened to Uncle Tommy's Monte Carlo all those years ago. For years, the official version was that "someone must've hit it and taken off." A nasty hit-and-run. A mystery no one cared enough to investigate.

But a few beers in—after the carne asada smoke had softened our guilt and the music had loosened our tongues—the truth finally rolled out.

Mom would just stare at us like she was trying to rewind the last thirty years in her head. Dad shook his head, muttered something like "you two being lucky to still be alive," and then—because it was a cookout—took a long sip of his beer and laughed anyway.

Every gathering, whether inside or outside, felt like a celebration of us being us. Kitchens became stages. Dining rooms became banquet halls. Backyards became stadiums.

Through the noise, the spills, the overcooked potatoes, the undercooked tamales—there was laughter, storytelling, and the unmistakable magic of family simply together.

Of course, other types of fun happened at these gatherings…

My nephew Junior had a pair of Airsoft pistols—the spring-loaded kind with a magazine that held maybe a dozen tiny plastic pellets. They looked like the real deal, but getting hit by one barely counted as violence. A quick sting, maybe a yelp if you were dramatic, and then a warm little tingle at the "wound site" for a minute or two. Nothing that could stop a barbecue.

Junior would lay empty beer bottles on their sides inside a big cardboard box—the mouths facing us like they were daring someone to try. The challenge? Shoot a pellet into the mouth of the bottle from twenty paces. Not an easy task sober… and infinitely more entertaining with a little alcohol in the bloodstream.

As it was, those Airsoft pistols weren't exactly engineered for precision. Add to that the slowly blurring vision, the swaying stance, and the sudden realization that the target kept moving (even though it definitely wasn't), and you had a recipe for some world-class terrible marksmanship.

On generous nights, when everyone was feeling bold and a little overconfident, five-dollar bets would go down. Winner takes all. Bragging rights included. Whoever managed to arc a single pellet into the mouth of that beer bottle—usually by accident—walked away like they'd just won Olympic gold.

My dad got into the action once, and wouldn't you know it? On the very first try, he got one *in* the bottle. The sound it made as it hit home—a pure, resonant ping of plastic on glass—was impossible to deny.

He froze for a moment, savoring it, then slowly raised his arms, beer in one hand, Airsoft pistol in the other. For a heartbeat, he looked exactly like Doc Holliday in *Tombstone*—calm, confident, just a little dangerous, and completely owning the moment.

The rest of us cheered, laughed, and immediately conceded defeat. There was no coming back from that.

It wasn't just a game. It was cookout physics.

Cookout skill.

Cookout science.

Somehow, as we all live our lives apart, the best times always come back to the table. The small, intimate meals, where everyone's elbows are touching, where stories are shared, and where laughter fills the space between bites.

Years later, we may gather at Denny's or some other diner, the pancakes never quite as good as Mom's tortillas, the coffee never quite as strong.

But the family time remains rich. The conversations, inevitably, circle back to the legends of our youth—the tales of mischief, triumph, and absurdity that somehow shaped who we are.

And of Mom… I like to think she's watching us from heaven, smiling at the mess, the laughter, the love, and the stories. Because after all these years, she would have loved every chaotic, perfect, perfectly imperfect second of it.

For us, food wasn't just food.

It was memory.

It was theater.

It was comedy.

And it was our love language—spoken fluently, chaotically, and always with second helpings.

This was, and still is, the Flavor of Family.

STANDING GUARD

ITS ALL ABOUT THE BADGE

Standing Guard: It's All About the Badge

People think private security is all sunglasses, earpieces, and deep, meaningful nods—like we're one dramatic hallway walk away from starring in our own action movie. Hollywood did that to us.

Somewhere between Kevin Costner diving in front of Whitney Houston and Jason Statham beating up twelve men with a stapler, the world decided private security was basically law enforcement in slightly shinier khakis and worse dialogue.

Truth is, the closest thing Hollywood ever got to portraying us accurately was Paul Blart. And even he was hyped up—zipping around on a Segway like a kid on Halloween who just discovered sugar is a lifestyle, not a snack—and somehow thinks he's the hero of a blockbuster.

In real life, most security shifts are so quiet that a Segway would fall asleep under you.

Private security is 60% standing, 25% telling people "Sorry, you can't go in there," 10% trying not to fall asleep while standing, and 5% explaining—for the thousandth time—that no, you are not a police officer, detective, CIA operative, or "undercover secret agent of the greater mall jurisdiction."

Most of the job is a delicate balance between looking alert, deterring trouble, and pretending your feet aren't planning a mutiny—or that the stapler on the desk isn't plotting against you.

And the misconceptions?

Endless.

People assume you're either a superhero or a failed one. They think we're trained in twelve martial arts and have a tragic backstory that pushed us into the private sector. They imagine we're all ex-cops, ex-military, or ex-something impressive. Truth is, some of us are exes—but mostly ex–night shift workers who wanted a job where people occasionally brought donuts.

The media portrays private security as glamorous. Real life private security is:
"Hey, could you escort this slightly angry man who keeps trying to open a locked supply closet because he swears he left his 'important business folder' in there even though he doesn't work here?"

Private security isn't in the business of chasing bad guys.

We're in the business of preventing bad choreography—making sure the wrong people don't wander into the wrong rooms, bump into the wrong VIPs, or accidentally unplug the wrong equipment that costs more than our yearly salary.

Not that we have much of a choice, anyway.

Unless you're one of those overpaid celebrity bouncers with necks the size of tree trunks, job descriptions that include things like "stand there looking intimidating, retrieve the vegan smoothie without making eye contact, and maybe do a slow-motion hair flip while glaring at a paparazzo," the rest of us are operating in the realm of everyday nonsense.

Most private security gigs aren't dramatic. They just feel dramatic because your radio crackles once every forty-five minutes and you think it might finally be your moment—only to hear: "Unit 4, can someone check the women's restroom? There's a suspicious noise coming from the trash can."

Ah yes. Another crisis averted.

Another step closer to keeping the universe in balance.

Celebrity bouncers get yacht parties, VIP entrances, and $800 sneakers.

We get keys, clipboards, and people who swear the rules don't apply to them because they 'know the owner's cousin's former roommate.' But hey—someone's gotta keep the choreography clean.

I once lived the glamorous life of a private security guard. You wouldn't know that just by seeing me, but I must admit, it is true. No, really; It is.

I don't remember how I got my first gig or who referred me. It was after leaving the Marines (a fact I covered in a previous story, and yes—it's still classified). Somehow, civilian life had me trading combat boots for…well, slightly less comfortable boots, a uniform that made me look important, and a job description that basically read: "Stand here. Look serious. Nod occasionally."

The transition from Marine to mall-cop-adjacent reality was…let's say, eye-opening.

In the Marines, danger was usually loud, fast, and required strategy (well, not so much for me, but that's the story we tell).

In private security, danger was slow, polite, and often carried a shopping bag.

What I do remember is walking into the office of a guy named Alfonso. Lived in Brawley. Tall, maybe six feet, thick-rimmed glasses, a little cross-eyed. Nice enough. He introduced himself, handed me a stack of documents, waited for me to scribble my name everywhere, and then—without ceremony—handed me three uniform shirts.

"You're a medium, right?"
I asked about the bottoms.
"Just wear jeans."

Then he laminated my info onto a little card, slapped it down on the desk, and said, "This is your guard card. Keep it on you at all times."

Before I could even process that, he handed me a .22 pistol and a badge.

"The back of your card has your gun permit. If cops ask, just show 'em the card. They won't say anything."

In my mind, red flags were waving like it was Fiesta Mexicana. This can't be legit… right? But hey—this was a paying job.

And I must admit, the badge was cool as heck.

My first assignment? Night shift at the Coachella Canal Lining Project.
6:00 p.m. to 6:00 a.m.
A 90-mile drive there.
And a 90-mile drive back.

Upon arrival, I was to relieve the day guard, a man everyone called Don Rafa. Now that guy was a character straight out of a low-budget action movie. I'd pull up and find him sitting on top of his Chevy van: shirt unbuttoned, badge clipped to his belt, a .357 tucked into his waistband, a shotgun across his lap, cowboy hat pushed back, aviator sunglasses on, and—chef's kiss—an ice chest full of beers right next to him, because hydration in the desert is apparently optional—but style is mandatory.

Every movement of his seemed effortless—the way he cracked open a beer, the way he adjusted his shotgun, the casual tilt of his hat. He looked like he owned the desert, the van, and maybe even the stars above it. I didn't know whether to be impressed, terrified, or slightly envious. Probably all three at once.

Then he glanced at me, eyebrow raised, and offered a grin that said, “Welcome to your first night, kid. You’re gonna love it—or hate it. Maybe both.”

The job itself was simple. Mostly stay in your car. Every hour, hop out and do your rounds—check the perimeter gates, insert the key into the little metal clock box, turn it twice so it recorded the timestamp. Dangers? Coyotes, rattlesnakes, undocumented folks trying to slip north quietly, and the occasional couple looking for a dark, isolated place to do what couples do.

On the first day, Don Rafa interrogated me about everything—where I was from, who I knew, whether I had a girlfriend, whether I liked Tecate or Bud Light. Then he offered me a beer. Before he drove off, he asked:

“¡Ay mijo!” he wheezed between fits, slapping his knee like he’d just witnessed the best punchline of the decade. “With that thing, you’re gonna scare away what—field mice? Maybe a drunk rattlesnake?”

He wiped tears from his eyes and shook his head, still chuckling. To him, my little .22 probably looked like something you’d win at the Calexico carnival after sinking three plastic rings onto a milk bottle—more toy than tool. Meanwhile, he sat there armed like he was auditioning for the remake of *Desperado*.

Then, without warning, his laugh stopped. “You’d better take this.”

He took the .22, handed me the .357, and tossed me a box of rounds like he was trading marbles on the playground—except the marbles could ruin your life if dropped.

The thing felt heavy in my hands—too heavy—like it knew I had no business holding it. He leaned in, squinted at me over those scratched-up aviators, and said, dead serious, “Don’t point it at anything you’re not willing to patch up later. And if you hear a noise, don't go running toward it. That's how stupid people in movies die."

He let the words hang there, then added, almost as an afterthought, "And if something does go down, just remember—aim small, miss small. But mostly? Don't miss."

I nodded like I understood, even though my heartbeat was doing jumping jacks inside my chest.

I wanted to ask about the shotgun. I mean… wasn't the .357 enough firepower for one man sitting on top of a van in the middle of nowhere? He must've read my mind, because he grinned and said:

"The shotgun? That's for the coyotes. Those bastards'll come after you. One gets too close and—BAM!" Then he laughed like someone who had, in fact, BAM'd more than a few things in his lifetime.

"No te creas," he added, taking a long swig of his Budweiser. "I'm no good with the handgun. Shotgun's easier for me."

Of course it was.

Of course, the man who treated danger like a hobby preferred the loudest, most chaotic tool in the arsenal. He said it so casually—like someone announcing they preferred flour tortillas over corn.

And with that, he turned over the engine, revved it a couple of times just to assert dominance over the quiet afternoon, and eased the van toward the exit. The back bumper rattled like it was held on with prayers and zip ties.

"Allí te veo mañana," he called out through the open window, hand waving lazily as the van crawled away.

Entertainment on the job? The radio, the occasional nighttime visit from Border Patrol or the Sheriff's office… and me teaching myself guitar in the dead silence of the desert. Like something out of one of those old Westerns—minus the campfire.

We were stationed near the Chocolate Mountains. Around me, the desert stretched flat and empty. Coyotes yipped in the distance, their calls echoing off the ridges. Occasionally, the ground trembled from some far-off military explosive test—BOOM—no warning, just a reminder that you were alive… and very, very small.

The moonlight made everything look sharper, harsher. Shadows of scraggly brush and twisted mesquite trees stretched across the dirt, sometimes making me jump until I realized it was just a rock… or a very curious desert jackrabbit.

Twelve hours is a long time, and a man's gotta keep busy. So I played. Notes stumbled, chords rang wrong, but the music filled the silence, kept the night from swallowing me whole, and gave the desert a little company.

And so it went for a couple of months, until the canal lining was finally finished. And no, I didn't have to shoot a thing. Scout's honor.

After that, I was transferred closer to home—to the original Brawley Inn. The place had gone under financially and was officially closed, but the owners hired private security to keep watch. Apparently, the last manager had held onto his keys after being let go and would drop by from time to time to "liberate" hotel supplies. That's where I came in.

This job was cake. I had access to the diner, which the manager kept stocked with fresh coffee—and everything needed to brew more. I discovered—on my first night—exactly how much coffee one human can consume before they start seeing colors. Oh, and the shift came with a bonus: anything in the fridge was fair game.

Local sheriff's deputies made regular rounds.

Brawley PD dropped by.
Border Patrol.
Even Highway Patrol.
They all stopped in for coffee—and most brought donuts or burritos. *Score.*

They even offered to do my rounds for me, checking doors and the quad. A 12-hour shift with company, free breakfast, and no explosions? Not terrible at all.

There were occasional attempted break-ins, teens sneaking in to take a dip in the still-operating pool—or to smoke pot—and, yes, the same types of couples who used to disappear out to the dark isolation of the desert to do…what couples do. Every so often, these duos would quietly try to "secure a room" without checking in with me first. (You already know what this means, right?)

In other words, private security isn't always about chasing criminals. Sometimes it's about politely reminding people that, no, your romantic misadventures do not override the hotel's policy—and yes, I'm watching.

Once, a Brawley PD officer was having coffee, and in the middle of our conversation he nodded toward my bag and asked about my sidearm.

I blinked.
"My what?"
"Your piece! I see it in your bag. Mind if I take a look?"

Inside, I immediately thought: *Oh F***. I'm toast.*
Outside, I played it cool. "Oh! That."

I reached into my duffel, pulled it out, and handed it over. He checked the cylinder, inspected the frame, then closed one eye and aimed casually toward the diner door like he was picking out wallpaper.

"Nice," he finally said. "My backup piece is a .357." Then he handed it back like we were just two gun collectors comparing stamps.

Damn. No questions. If only he knew…

That gig lasted about two months. The owner sold off the business and the property and that was that. From there, the gigs were nothing more than overnight office sitting, construction site babysitting, and many, many parties.

There was a property that shall remain nameless (the statute of limitations may not have run out yet…no, I'm kidding, but still not telling you the name). This place had a number of empty warehouses, connected by a long, paved corridor running the length of the facility. Usually, there were four of us assigned to this area—for "safety reasons." More on that later.

It had a tiny office and a parking garage that used to house work trucks. By the time I arrived, it held five golf carts.

Yes, I know what you're thinking.

And yes, we did.

One night, out of sheer boredom, we closed the office and lined up the carts. Each of us took one.

"Want to put money on this?"

"Nah, man. Just for fun."

"Awe, no fun. I got a cool fifty that I take the win."

"I'll take that action."

"Alright. On the sound of the horn, we go."

“3… 2… 1…” (HONK)

And we took off. Let me tell you, these things could move—not screaming fast, but fast enough. Flying down that corridor as fast as the carts would go, with nothing but the glow of their blinking safety lights illuminating the way. Four dudes, our own nighttime quarter mile…with all the grace of a demolition derby rehearsed by toddlers.

The finish? Not what you probably have in mind. The far end of the corridor was dark, and I was pretty sure it ended in an elevated loading ramp. And sure enough…one of us (I won’t say who) met it head-on. Cart included. Pretty loud crash, too. Luckily, no one was injured. Can’t say the same about that poor cart.

“Shit! You okay, man?”

“Yeah…just a little spooked.”

“Yo, the bossman won’t be happy about this. How we gonna explain it?”

Thinking quickly, I said, “I got it.” And this is where the “safety” thing comes in:

“You know how they’re always saying we gotta keep an eye out for trespassers? We can just say a bunch of teens broke in late at night and were joyriding on the carts. That’s what happened.”

“Yeah! And they ran off when they heard us coming.”

NOTE: There were no cameras back then—at least not at this place. No one would’ve been wiser. And it worked. They bought it. By the next shift, the carts were chained down. I guess that was the end of our little midnight Grand Prix.

This assignment, too, was short-lived. The property was sold off, the warehouses demolished, and the land eventually redeveloped into housing.

From there, I was assigned to parties and celebrations. Most halls back then required security for quinceaneras and receptions (most still do). So it was patrolling the outside of salones and parking lots while people partied.

One of the most memorable gigs I had was a huge block party in Brawley. It was a cul-de-sac, and all the neighbors got together for a Fourth of July blowout—just like you see on TV. Tables lined the street, food everywhere, and of course, alcohol. Carne asada, burgers and hotdogs, ribs, colitas…even a Budweiser beer truck with four taps at the closed end of the street.

They hired six of us to patrol the event and keep unwanted guests out. It was as rowdy as you'd expect, but mostly went off without incident. Jose, the "lead" guard, was everywhere at once—giving directions, schmoozing guests, basically working the party like he owned it.

And, as Fourth of July parties tend to go, fireworks were going off pretty much the entire time.

But the *real* fireworks started when Jose's on-again, off-again girlfriend Gina showed up. She also worked security and had just finished another gig—still in uniform.

Gina was the jealous type (explains the repeated breakups). She spotted Jose chatting up one of the ladies, beer in hand, and her temper ignited like a bottle rocket in a fireworks store. A fight broke out.

I was at the far end of the street, thinking it was some drunk guest scuffle.

Nope.

By the time I reached them, they were both on the ground, slightly bloody—and yet the party went on like nothing had happened. Cops were called, and both were taken away. Alfonso, our boss, showed up later and just shrugged.

Apparently, this had happened before at other assignments, and yes—they were both going to be fired. Again. (Somehow, they always got rehired—guess not many people want this "glamorous" job.)

Later, I was told Jose had been stabbed by Gina, and he punched her unconscious in retaliation.

The party? Totally lit.

Chaos, blood, fireworks—classic Fourth of July, right?

And that, in a very long, meandering, slightly chaotic nutshell, is what private security looks like when the cameras aren't rolling and the Segways are asleep (At least here in the valley).

It's equal parts boredom, caffeine, mild danger, and improvisation. We are the silent choreographers of everyday chaos, the unsung referees of drunken logic, the polite reminders that policies exist even if your cousin's roommate once met the owner's dog.

No Hollywood script could capture it—the long drives, the empty corridors, the golf cart derbies, the desert jackrabbits, or the occasional Fourth of July fistfight.

And honestly? That's probably for the best. Because if anyone ever did try to dramatize it, they'd leave out the small victories: keeping a teen out of a pool, preventing a couple from accidentally redecorating a hotel room, or teaching yourself guitar in the middle of nowhere just to survive the silence.

We don't get trophies or cinematic slow-motion walkaways. Sometimes our adrenaline comes from spotting a rattlesnake before it spots you, or from realizing that no, this shift didn't require shooting anything—or anyone. Most of the time, we get to sip coffee, nod politely, and quietly hold the line between chaos and… slightly less chaos.

And, admittedly, sometimes falling asleep.

And honestly? That's enough. Because in private security, the true glory isn't in the chase or the shootouts—it's in the little absurd victories, the small wins nobody applauds, and the stories we get to tell afterward.

So, if you ever see a guard standing quietly in a hallway, sunglasses perched on their nose, nodding like they're part of some epic narrative—you now know the truth. They're probably thinking about their next coffee refill, checking the trash can for suspicious noises, and quietly remembering the time a golf cart nearly killed someone.

And maybe, just maybe, they're smiling at the absolute absurdity of it all.

Welcome to private security.

Not glamorous.

Not heroic.

Perfectly ridiculous—and absolutely real.

A Little Art,
A Little Play,
A Lot of L.A.

A Little Art, a Little Play, a Lot of L.A.

Growing up, I was always doodling on everything. Heck, my textbooks and notebooks were more graffiti than notes. College?

Didn't think it was for me right out of high school. While everyone else was plotting ways to fatten their futures, I took the scenic route. Went rogue. Enlisted in the Marine Corps.

The rest of that story? Classified. Need-to-know. And you don't need to know… not yet, anyway.

Life after the Corps… well, let's just say a handful of odd jobs and a stint as a day camp leader eventually pushed me toward trying to get a degree in art. I mean, what the heck? Gotta do something, right?

Imperial Valley College came first. My first semester was, shall we say… a very successful failure. I didn't really want to be there, so I signed up for whatever courses made the schedule easiest. I had a very "nice" meeting with my guidance counselor, who reminded me—quite powerfully—how spectacularly I was failing at college.

But there was a silver lining. That's when I met the man who would become my mentor in the arts: Dr. Capet. Interesting guy. A little eccentric—always pacing the room, giving direction, scribbling notes in the margins of a sketchbook no one else would touch, or quietly working on some piece of his own—but somehow, he was relatable. He had this way of seeing the world sideways, and somehow, he made it feel like seeing it sideways was exactly the way you were supposed to see it.

By my second semester, I'd signed up for every class he offered, like a kid who'd discovered a candy store and decided to sample everything. And along the way, I met some fascinating people—creatives who were as obsessed, as talkative, as endlessly curious as Lefty, Virginia, and, now, myself. It was the kind of environment where ideas bounced off the walls so fast you almost needed a helmet.

It wasn't just learning—it was being plugged into a world that felt like it had always existed just beyond my reach, waiting for me to find it.

Lefty Martin.

Legend.

He was a beautiful soul, the kind who made even the dusty Valley afternoons feel a little lighter. You never knew if it was the way he laughed or the way he spun a story, but somehow, he made everything feel easier, like troubles shrank a little in his orbit.

I remember it like it was yesterday: walking into class and seeing that the only seat left was next to him. Lefty was imposing at first glance—broad shoulders, that calm stillness of someone who saw more than he ever said—but there was a gentleness to him you felt before he ever opened his mouth.

He was working on a colored-pencil portrait of Redd Foxx, humming softly as he shaded in the lines, coaxing expression out of paper like it was the most natural thing in the world. The likeness was so good it stopped me in my tracks. I was instantly impressed, and I think he noticed—not in a proud way, but in that quiet Lefty way, where acknowledgment came in a nod, a grin, a slight lift of the eyebrow that said, *Yeah… I see you too.* He looked at me, smiled, and said, "Have a seat, young man. I'm Lefty. Let's see what you've got."

I was working on a black-and-white stippled portrait of Eddie Van Halen—tiny dots covering the page, with a million more waiting. He took one look and said, "Ooooooo! That's fire! I'm gonna have to learn to do that."

And just like that, we started talking. It didn't take much—just a comment about how he got Redd Foxx's eyes to look like they were about to deliver a punchline—and suddenly we were off.

Lefty had that gift. Conversations with him didn't start so much as happen, like you'd been talking for years and simply picked up where you left off.

I blame him for getting me into colored pencils. Truly. Up until then, it had always been graphite and ink for me—safe, predictable, the tools I knew how to control. But after Lefty, a whole new world opened up. Color. Actual color. He made it look easy, like all you had to do was pick up a red or a blue and trust your hand to know what to do.

I remember watching him work and thinking, Man… I want to do that. And Lefty, without ever making a big deal about it, nudged me right into it. A recommendation here, a tip there, a "Try this shade, you'll see" tossed over his shoulder. Next thing I knew, I was standing in front of the art supply aisle like I'd discovered some secret portal.

And then there was Virginia—a fellow creative, sharp-eyed and always carrying at least three ideas at once. She slipped into our orbit so naturally it felt like she'd always been there. Just like that, the three of us became a trio of overactive, talkative,

restless makers, turning any classroom corner or quiet patch of campus into our own studio.
We weren't just drawing; we were *plotting*, experimenting, comparing colors, trading sketches, laughing too loud, and dreaming even louder. Lefty brought the calm skill, Virginia brought the fire, and I… well, I bounced somewhere in between, trying to keep up with both of them and loving every chaotic minute of it.

Those were the days when creativity felt endless—when a pencil, a scrap of paper, and a half-formed idea were all we needed to feel like we were building whole worlds.

I have no idea how it happened, but at some point we became… well, I'm not even sure how to put it—the driving force of creativity in that class.

Always challenging each other (artistically, of course), trading stories, offering critiques, pushing ideas further. And Dr. Capet noticed. "Laughter? Laughter? Stop that!" he'd call out. Not mean, just his way of engaging, of relating. I think he genuinely liked us. He even once told us we were closer to him than his own nieces and nephews.

While everyone else was busy at work—or at least pretending to be—there we were: creating, laughing, sharing supplies, just… being artists. And that, I realized, is what we artist types do.

The next couple of years passed in a blur. The three of us—Lefty, Virginia, and me—were in almost every class together. Sometimes, we weren't even officially enrolled; we were just there for the creative space, the freedom to make, to experiment, to throw ideas at the wall and see what stuck.

Creatives need other creatives around. We steal inspiration from each other.

I discovered new mediums to work with, and I met a second professor who nudged my artistic trajectory: Kate Rapp. Demanding. (And a little mean.) But boy, did she push you past your limits—or rather, shove you right out of them.
She taught Drawing from Life, inventing exercises that felt like a strange mix of torture and revelation. My favorites—eventually—were the “burns” and the non-dominant hand exercises. Favorite now, hated them to death then. There was something about struggling to draw with your left hand or being forced to rework a piece until it bled personality you didn’t think you had that left you exhausted, exhilarated, and just a little terrified.

But that was the point. Every grumble, every groan, every frustrated sigh was part of the process. She didn’t coddle talent; she *demanded* growth. And somehow, in the middle of all that chaos, I learned more than I ever thought possible.

The burns were nothing more than rapid-sketch exercises. We’d head out into the quad, she’d give us fifteen seconds to capture whatever we saw. Three rules: the drawing tool must never leave the page, no erasing, and fill the page. “Burn ’em up,” she’d say.

Thirty minutes once a week, and somehow, by the end, you could see your eye and hand syncing in ways you hadn’t thought possible.

The non-dominant hand exercises were even more fun—if you define “fun” as torture. We’d tape a marker to the end of a yardstick and draw with our non-dominant hand at arm’s length. Giant sketch pads could be on an easel or on the floor.
Either way, it was… a workout. But it built your vision, your control, your confidence for drawing in ways nothing else could.

Painful? Absolutely.

Worth it? Without a doubt.

At some point, it was time to move on. Everything reaches that point. I graduated from IVC with an Associate's Degree in Studio and Fine Arts and transferred to art school at UCLA.
Talk about culture shock.
There I was—small-town me, technically skilled, introverted—stepping into a world where the artist types seemed to spend half their time talking about their art and the other half contemplating actually making it. It was overwhelming, exciting… and completely, utterly different from anything I'd known.

It was like this world—pardon the expression—*"half-assed"* some art and then talked endlessly about it. Every possible meaning, every hidden metaphor, every emotional nuance. How they got there, why they made that choice, and where the piece might be "leading" next.

Meanwhile, I'd be standing there thinking, *Dude… it's just an apple.*

I remember someone even saying it was "pure performance," and honestly, that was the thing about that place: you couldn't just make art. You had to talk about the art. A lot. The commentary was half the assignment and maybe three-quarters of the culture.

Not something I was used to.

Up there, it was all cheese, wine, thoughtful nodding, and conversations that lasted longer than the actual painting sessions. And there I was—tucked into my little corner of the world, flinging paint, snapping photos, doing my best imitation of someone who belonged there, all while trying to make sense of this big, strange, exciting universe I'd stumbled into.

That's when I discovered the 8th floor. The art building had eight floors, and the top one—the lofts—was something else entirely. Big, open spaces, floor-to-ceiling bay windows, and a view of the Hollywood Hills that could steal your breath if you weren't careful.

To my surprise, it was rarely used. Always open in the mornings. Naturally, I signed up. I shared the space with a couple of other painters, though they hardly painted. Mostly they sat around, talked, played guitar, and ate. And there was always food.

I set up my stuff permanently by the windows. Gorgeous view. Endless light. My safe space. A little slice of calm in a place that otherwise seemed to thrive on chaos, wine, and conversation.

Every now and then, I'd venture down into the Sculpture Garden—a five-acre, open-air space on campus with over seventy modern and contemporary sculptures.

Designed as a place where art and nature could mingle, it had a formal brick plaza, a walkway lined with coral trees, and winding lawns with curving paths. I'd wander through it, sketchbook in hand, doing burns (remember those? yeah, still love 'em).

And that's where I met the famous UCLA squirrels. Thieves and beggars, if you ask me. You'd be sitting there, sandwich, chips, or other snacks in hand, and one of these little cuties would crawl up, stand before you, cock its head to one side, and… put out both tiny paws, as if asking for a bite. Cute, right?

But some weren't so charming. The little bastards worked in teams, crawling close with all the charm in the world, then—bam!—make off with your sandwich before you even realized what happened. I quickly learned: in the Sculpture Garden, you share the space with art, nature… and a highly organized squirrel crime syndicate.

It was also at UCLA where I learned why the term "starving artist" was coined. Art is expensive, and it doesn't always pay for itself. Sure, I sold a painting here and there, but nothing serious. I needed a reliable funding source.

Financial aid and work study covered some expenses, so I landed a job with UCLA's coffee service. Simple gig, really: show up early, grab the list of orders, load up the van, and deliver. Most days the van was already packed. Deliveries went to offices all over campus, and once a week I'd service the machines. Eight hours of pay, five days a week, but most days only three or four hours of actual work—sometimes as little as ninety minutes.

The job had perks. I got to learn how the university worked and explore the various offices. The Medical Campus was especially cool. Those researchers consumed coffee like it was oxygen.

There was one office—two doctors, four assistants, strictly research—that ordered fifteen cases of Farmer Brothers Colombian coffee per week. Each case had forty-eight pods, each pod making sixteen cups. That's… a lot of coffee.

The job was great—until "restructuring" reassigned it to UCLA Food Services. Good while it lasted, though. And honestly? It kept me fed, caffeinated, and able to keep painting.

I would walk to work from my apartment just off campus, taking a short trail through the woods—a little shortcut to UCLA. This was a daily ritual most mornings, between school and work.

Afternoons? Not so much. The trail was alive: crisp air tinged with dew, the faint perfume of wildflowers and damp earth, and the whispering leaves of eucalyptus and oak. Birds called from the canopy above, and the path seemed to move with you, a rhythm all its own.

And then there was the spider web. The largest I'd ever seen—at least seven feet tall and six feet wide—strung like delicate steel between two trees. Morning sunlight would peek through

the leaves, catching each silky thread so it glimmered like spun glass against the dark shadows of the forest. And smack in the middle? The spider. No clue what kind—it was the big kind, the kind that made you stop dead in your tracks. I nearly walked right into it more than once. I just happened to look up at the right moment and caught the sunlight glinting off the web. There it was, perfectly centered, staring back like it owned the trail.
I always wondered what happened in the afternoons—did someone accidentally walk into it, or take it down on purpose? I always wanted to photograph it, but mornings were rushed, and when I did manage to snap a photo, I never had the settings just right to get a good shot. Ah, the life of an apprentice.

One morning, running late for work, I grabbed what I thought was a can of Coke. Halfway up the trail, thirsty, I cracked it open and took a huge swig…

UUUUGGGGH.

What the heck? This is beer. Tecate, to be exact.
(See, children? This is why you don't rush through life and make "last minute" decisions.)

Part of my studies at UCLA included photography. I bought a vintage all-metal Canon AE-1 and a couple of lenses, learned to develop film, and print my own photos. Time in the chemical labs was… kind of dull and lonely. Just you, your photos, and that depressing amber light.

Our professor drilled one lesson into us above all else: Shoot all the time. "Good shooters take their camera everywhere. Shoot all the time," he'd say. So I did. I carried my camera everywhere, along with a handful of extra rolls of film—yes, film. This was before digital.

One day, heading back to my apartment, I passed the Men's Gym. They often hosted basketball games between the college team, retired pros, and up-and-coming players. That's where I met Shaquille O'Neal. Star-struck doesn't even begin to cover it. That was one big dude.

Magic Johnson was there, too, along with the O'Bannon brothers. They'd just finished a few pick-up games and were outside signing autographs and chatting with fans. And then there was me… camera hanging around my neck, extra rolls of film in my bag… and damn it, I completely forgot to snap a photo.

Dumbass.

My time at UCLA was also when I discovered—or shall I say, rediscovered—Mariachi music. I grew up with it, and I knew of it, but it was here that I really learned to play. My roommate (and cousin), Juan, was part of Mariachi UCLA. When I moved up there, he asked if I wanted to tag along.

I started by attending the Mariachi class on campus: Ethnomusicology 91K—Music of Mexico. And the professors? None other than Nati Cano and Jesus "Chuy" Guzman of the world-renowned Mariachi Los Camperos. Being in that class, learning from them, was like stepping into a whole new world—and, at the same time, reconnecting with a part of my roots I hadn't fully appreciated until then.

Pretty soon, I was practicing with Mariachi UCLA—and then gigging. Fun times. And extra pocket cash.

Driving to and from gigs was an adventure. Sometimes it meant long stretches of freeway, snacks in hand, navigating Los Angeles with a battered Thomas Guide—the pre-GPS survival manual for anyone trying not to get hopelessly lost.

Performing was its own circus. Most of the time, it was backyard parties, church masses, small reception halls, and the occasional stage show. Weddings, birthdays, quinceañeras, family reunions, divorce celebrations (yes, these do happen), funerals…

basically anything that could be celebrated, we were there. Add alcohol, and things got really fun—sometimes chaotic, sometimes downright ridiculous, but always unforgettable.

Each gig came with its own little circus: the uneven backyard lawn, the echoey church nave, the cramped reception hall with folding chairs lined too close together. But somehow, no matter the chaos, the music carried us through, and somehow, we all survived with our instruments, our dignity… mostly intact.

And yet, there was a rhythm to it, a camaraderie that made it feel like family. The music, the jokes, the shared near-disasters—everything blended together into a sensory overload that was surprisingly addictive. That was gigging life: messy, loud, unpredictable… and absolutely unforgettable.

I loved every minute of it.

You tend to meet some interesting people when gigging. Case in point: it was through a Mariachi gig that I came to meet the original Gomez Addams—John Astin.

No, seriously.

True story.

The story goes like this: one of our violin players was working toward her doctorate and did much of her work with UCLA's Education Department. Alexander Astin, the founding director of the Higher Education Research Institute at UCLA, hired the group for a party at his Malibu home. I had no clue who the man was. But he looked so familiar.

I recall sitting there between sets. He was at the piano, just tinkering. I guess he felt me staring because he turned toward me, smiled, and said, "I know what you're thinking. I'm not him. He'll be along in a little bit," and winked.

And like clockwork, in walked John Astin—Gomez Addams himself—cigar in hand, same goofy but charming smile from TV. Really down-to-earth, surprisingly approachable. And there was me again… completely star-struck. Probably wearing a goofy smile myself.

Art school was fun, but the experiences *around* the work? LA is a place where you can do pretty much anything. There's something for everyone, and everyone has a "fun" story to tell. I am no different.

For me, the most embarrassing moment happened on what my roommates called the "only one beer" night. The first six months in LA, I generally stayed away from big parties—and certainly any alcohol (no, really). My roommates would ask if I wanted to go along for a drink, and I would decline. On occasion, I even served as the designated driver.

But eventually, my excuses ran out. My birthday was coming up. So they said, "Let's go to Malone's. Have a drink." I was all like, "Nah, man."

"Come on, man," they insisted. "Just one drink. ONE!"

"JUST ONE?" I asked, suspicious.

"Yeah. Just one!" they said.

"Ok… but just one," I warned.

Ok. So we all got ready. Malone's was just a few blocks away, a short walk. The place was packed—college kids blowing off steam, video screens on almost every wall, music blaring.
"Alright, a toast!" my cousin Juan said. "To Mariano, for finally having *one drink* with us."

And that's when I knew I was done for.

They handed me the *one drink*: a tall, 48-ounce glass mug of Killian's Irish Red. My roommate Angel said, "You said *ONE beer*. This is ONE beer. You can't back out now, man!"

Nimodo. A chingarle. This was the *ONE* beer I agreed to.

"Cheers!"

Took a big swig. A little bitter, ice-cold. Not terrible. Not wanting to be the odd man out, I kept pace with the rest of the bunch. Ten minutes later, the mug was empty.

That familiar fuzzy feeling started creeping up my nose. Everything around me began to lag, move slow. Next thing I knew, I was looking at the floor—and it was wet. Angel grabs me: "Dude, let's get him out of here before anyone notices."

Juan is laughing his ass off.

They got me up the stairs and out into the cold, and bam—I started feeling really dizzy. "Let's get him some food, and then we can get him back home," they said.

So there we were, walking the one block to Fatburger. The smell of burgers settled my stomach, and I took a bite. For a brief instant, I felt a little normal again. Then… bam. That nauseous *up and out* feeling overcame me.

I bolted from the place, turned the corner, and released the demons. Juan came up behind me, sees me hunched over, and says, "Shit! Not in the car!" Too late. Round two hit me with vengeance.

A couple minutes later, Angel shows up, burgers in a paperbag.

"Did he… just… in the car?"

"Yup," Juan said.

"Damn, dude. Let's get him home… and away from here before the owner comes out."

That car, my friends, was a topless roadster. Leather seats. No idea who it belonged to. And we were *not* going to hang around to find out.
I don't really remember any of this story. I was informed the next day, over a hangover breakfast, as my friends recounted the chaos with a mix of laughter and disbelief.

"One beer," they said.

Right.

Well, technically, it was *one beer*.

The Laserium show at the Griffith Observatory was something else—a full-on Pink Floyd experience with synchronized light and laser effects. You'd recline in planetarium chairs while laser artists painted the dome ceiling with swirling graphics and patterns. Immersive, multi-sensory, a hallucinogenic rite of passage if you will.

Coincidentally, it was also the first time I got stoned. Honest—it wasn't on purpose. Somehow, once the lights went down and the show began, people started lighting up. How they snuck it in is beyond me, but in it went.

Soon enough, everyone in the dome was feeling the effects, which made the show feel even more intense. Colors stretched, patterns danced, and the music hit you in a way that was almost physical.

Afterwards, we went for a drive down Hollywood Boulevard looking for food. LA traffic, as always, was brutal, so we parked and hoofed it for a while. New York-style pizza, street vendor hot dogs, flashing signs, neon lights, the smell of exhaust and food mingling—everything hitting the senses at once. Still nursing a bit of a high, we made the best of it, taking it all in, grinning like fools at the chaos and magic of the city.

At one point, we came across some… *ladies.*

If you know, you know.
Shapely figures, as one might expect. And, of course, as surely as the sun rises, one of our crew started making comments. Dares started flying. Money was even laid out for the first to "make contact."

One of us—won't say who—stepped forward, trying to start a conversation.

"Hey, baby. What's up?"

She—or so we thought—turned around.

Uhm… that's not a she. She's got a beard.

Cue instant laughter. From us. From them.

"Don't be afraid, baby! This is Hollywood. Anything goes!"

More laughter.

Nervous laughter.
No more words. We all just turned around and headed back the other way.

And so that's how it went. A little work, a little art, a little Mariachi, and a little play.

Life has a nice rhythm to it.

There were times when, instead of heading up to the loft, I'd drive out to Venice and set up at the beach. That was the intent, anyway. Not exactly an easy place to focus—at least not for a neurodivergent, hyperactive weirdo like me. I tried the photography thing there too. Mixed results. Mostly, I ended up just hanging out, watching the waves, and eating snacks.

Mariachi brought more than just weekend gigs. Occasionally, stage shows would come along, and one of the most memorable was a Cinco de Mayo performance in partnership with the UCLA Folkloric Group.

It was more than just a stage show. The event kicked off in the early afternoon with a food festival alongside a gallery exhibit of traditional Mexican art. The smell of fresh tortillas, sizzling carne asada, steaming tamales, mole, and sweet pan dulce mingled with the vibrant sounds of music and folklórico dancing.

Walking through the crowd, you could feel the energy pulsing: children darting between booths, dancers swaying in colorful skirts, and the laughter of families celebrating together.

Later that evening, on stage, we played—adding our voices and instruments to the rhythms of the folkloric dancers, each note bouncing through the open-air courtyard. It wasn't just a performance—it was a full sensory experience, a celebration of culture, community, and music.

Still, between Mariachi and my art, I had to work. I followed the Coffee Service over to Food Services, and, much to the chagrin of my parents, I eventually dropped out of school and went full-time as a cook. The pay was good, and I chose the morning schedule—done by 2:00 p.m.—plenty of time to run errands, get stuff done, and still sneak up to the 8th-floor lofts for some painting. No one was keeping tabs.

My colleagues at the restaurant were interesting too. Most of them kept second jobs to make a little extra cash to send back home—Guatemala, Oaxaca, and other parts of Mexico. And oh, did they know how to party. Notorious for big shindigs and a seemingly superhuman tolerance for alcohol, they worked hard and played harder, and I quickly learned to respect both sides of that equation.

Two occasions stand out as especially noteworthy with this wild bunch.

The first was the El Parián incident. My Mariachi group had been hired to play at this new little restaurant trying to make a name for itself. A lot of groups had a *planta*—a regular spot where they served as the house music—and El Parián was hoping we might become theirs.

It was small, but charming. Warm lights, colorful tiles, that faint smell of limón and grilled meat lingering in the air. The gig was supposed to be four hours with half-hour breaks between sets. Easy enough.

We get there, tune up, adjust our trajes, and step onto the little stage—only to find the place completely empty. Totally. Except for one guy at the bar nursing a beer like it was his emotional support animal.

Still, the show must go on.
So we start.

Halfway through the set, only three customers have wandered in, and two of them look like they came in by accident. The owner comes up to our director and says he's cutting us off at one hour.

"Nimodo… no hay gente."

"Hey, I've got an idea," I said. "Let me make a phone call."

So I step off stage, ask the bartender if I can use the phone (remember, landlines), and call my buddy from Food Services. I tell him the situation. He laughs and says he'll come over—*and* bring a few friends.

Our set ends. The owner offers us a meal before we go. We sit, eat, watch the clock. Thirty minutes pass. Still only the same three customers.

"The night's over, guys. I guess it's time to go."

We start walking out… and that's when people begin to arrive.

My cook buddies from work stroll in like they own the place. They head straight to the bar, order beers, and—loud enough for the owner to hear—ask,

"¿A qué hora empieza el mariachi?"

Then another half dozen walk in. Same thing.

Then another group.

And another.

Next thing we know, the place is packed—wall-to-wall packed—with line cooks, prep cooks, dishwashers, bartenders, and waiters from every corner of L.A. Apparently my buddy called a few people… who called a few people… who called a few more. And every single one of them was a drinker.

The owner rushes over:
"¡Muchachos, por favor, se quedan otro rato, sí?"

The place gets *lit*.

Beers flowing.

Shots—*lots* of shots.

Music blasting.

People singing over us, dancing between tables, yelling requests.

We ended up playing straight through until closing—about 1:30 a.m.—and the place had never made so much money. The owner was thrilled. We were exhausted. And my cook buddies? They were just getting started.

The other occasion was *Coronita Night* at some dive near downtown—one of those places where the neon sign flickers, the jukebox sticks, and the bartender looks like he's seen every bad decision ever made within a five-mile radius.

Coronita Night meant $1 seven-ounce beers. *All. Night. Long.* Which, to my coworkers, was basically an invitation from God.

It was me and four friends from work.
I was the designated driver—*for good reason,* as you'll soon see.

I'll cut to the chase.

We were there for maybe three hours, tops. I ordered a Coke and a burger—classic safe choices when you know you're responsible for getting four half-civilized adults home alive. They ordered a wing platter and a round of Coronitas to start. The show had just begun—some local band with more ambition than tuning skills.

By the end of the night, when the check arrived, the damage was… impressive.

Wings: about twenty-five bucks

One bottomless Coke: $1.50

The beer? *Three hundred and thirty dollars.*

For 7oz Coronitas.

For four guys.

Four.

That's roughly a small kiddie pool of beer, if you do the math.

And this, my friends, is exactly why I was the designated driver.

The looks on their faces when they saw that bill?

Priceless.

The drive home? Silent—except for the sound of four grown men regretting every life choice that led them to a dive bar with $1 beers on a Thursday night.

So in the end, my L.A. education was about 40% art, 30% mariachi, 20% food service… and the remaining 10% split between accidental intoxication, celebrity encounters I failed to photograph, and Coronita bills large enough to fund a small government program.

Art school gave me technique, sure—but life around it gave me stories.

And in the end, that turned out to be the real masterpiece.

No regrets, though.

Well—maybe the topless roadster incident.

The Things We Hold On To

The Things We Hold On To…

We all have them—those little things we collect, keep, and sometimes worship. Trinkets, collectibles, random objects that somehow find their way onto our desks or shelves, quietly asserting their importance. Memorabilia, of course, but more than that: tiny monuments to memory.

When you think about it, it's funny—the things we decide are worth keeping.

Some things we keep are just trinkets—small, ordinary, maybe even silly. A figurine from a vacation, a keychain from a fast-food chain, a coin found on the street.

They don't mean much to anyone else, but to us, they carry a whisper of memory, a touch of a moment we're not ready to forget.

Grandparents and parents are particularly dangerous in this regard. Step into their homes, and it's like entering a museum curated over decades.

Each item—a photograph, a plate, a coin—tells a story. You almost feel like an archaeologist sifting through layers of history, carefully noting which treasures survived the passage of time. (And silently judging the Tupperware situation.)

Other things are more than trinkets—they're memorabilia. They have weight. My Uncle Tommy's collection of old vinyl records isn't just a bunch of albums; his collection of 'Oldies But Goodies' is a curated history of teenage heartbreaks, dance halls, and the songs that shaped generations.

Some treasures are tactile. Mom's *metate* and *molcajete* sit patiently in the kitchen—reminders of the meals that built a home, the rhythms of family life, the slow transformation of corn and spices into something sacred. Both are family relics, passed down through generations, each with a story to tell.

Baby clothes, once tiny enough to fit in your palm, now folded in boxes as reminders of how quickly time slips away.

Coins, shiny and dull, foreign and familiar, little tokens of journeys both literal and metaphorical.

Photo albums, of course, are their own kind of magic. Hundreds of photographs carefully glued onto stiff pages: family portraits, birthday parties, road trips, the random chaos of everyday life.

And of course, thrown in for good measure, are those pictures no one remembers taking or knows exactly where they were taken—but somehow they always manage to fit whatever story is being told.

We hold on to things because they remind us who we were when we first touched them. A flower pressed between the pages of a book can carry more weight than it should—one from a first prom, pinned crookedly to a borrowed jacket and saved afterward like proof that the night really happened. Another from a wedding, lifted gently from a table once the music stopped, still faintly scented with promises.

There are flowers tied to beginnings too, from the day a child was born, when everything felt new and terrifying and perfect all at once.

And then there are the last ones—the flowers laid down when words no longer work, dried and kept not to remember the goodbye, but to remind us that love bloomed there once… and that it still does, even after time tries to convince us otherwise.

Nowadays, everything ends up on Facebook or Instagram, mixed in with carefully staged snapshots of food nobody will ever admit to obsessively photographing—everyone does it.

Don't try to hide it. You know who you are. But the essence is the same: a desire to hold on.

Trinkets or memorabilia—they exist on a spectrum. Some are playful, some sacred, but all are attempts to hold onto what we love, who we were, and where we've been.

We hold on because these objects, silly or sacred, connect us to the people we love, the places we've been, and the selves we were—and in doing so, they help us navigate the selves we are.

We all have things we've held on to, perhaps longer than we should have.

Sure, there are those special things that have deep ties to our family's past, heirlooms that have been passed down, sometimes for generations. But we all have that box or drawer where we keep trinkets, things that perhaps won't mean much to anyone else.

Not the useful stuff—no one ever gets misty-eyed about an old stapler or a perfectly functional sweater. (Although I do know a couple of teachers who would absolutely contradict that statement—*vigorously*—and yes, one of them is my wife. You know I love you, right?)

No, the items we sometimes treasure most are the tiny, impractical, borderline ridiculous trinkets that somehow become emotional landmines.

Aside from photos, we cling to the small things: jewelry, coins, figurines, artesanías from that trip you barely remember, baby clothes that no longer fit even your memories, little folded notes from crushes that said absolutely nothing of substance… and yet meant everything at the time.

These are the artifacts that survive every spring cleaning, every move, every "I swear I'm going to declutter this year" false promise. You pick one up and instantly tumble through a wormhole into another version of yourself—a younger one, usually with worse hair and more optimism.

Some of these treasures were gifts. Others were traded, inherited, or found at the bottom of a drawer you didn't know existed.

And a few were… well… liberated (because your cousin didn't really need that tiny pewter mini-mariachi as much as you did. And look—you gave it a better life.)

I was looking through some boxes in my garage the other day—doing that seasonal ritual where you convince yourself you're going to "declutter" and "open up some space." You know, the lies we tell ourselves.

Man… box after box, I'm finding things. Little pieces of my past. Artifacts. Relics. Evidence that at some point in my life I was either sentimental, forgetful, or a borderline hoarder. Maybe all three. (And probably a fourth if you count my irrational attachment to broken pencils.)

It felt less like cleaning and more like conducting an archaeological dig. If Indiana Jones had grown up in Calexico, instead of discovering ancient temples, he would've discovered a cracked shoebox filled with 1980s marbles, a faded Van Halen button, and a mixtape labeled "Calexicali — DO NOT ERASE."

Every box was a time capsule. And every item inside was its own tiny memory grenade.

There was the jewelry—well, calling it "jewelry" is generous. More like tangled necklaces, the cheap, homemade kind from high school, and a ring I won from a 25-cent machine at Kmart.

Tangled in that mess were the rings Lisa and I had made, our names etched into the bands, the date we started dating engraved inside—just a few handfuls of years ago (I'm being generous here, don't judge)—yet somehow a lifetime of memories was wrapped up in that small circle of metal.

Coins too. Foreign coins, old pesos, a silver bicentennial quarter I swear was going to make me rich one day. And the arcade tokens—from Roundtable Pizza in the '80s—still sticky with ancient soda residue. You don't throw out an arcade token.

That's like throwing away your childhood muscle memory.

Then came the figurines—little artesanías my parents bought from a gas-station stand somewhere between Calexico and San Felipe. A ceramic set of portly little mariachis my parents gifted me many moons ago. They now live in a box in the garage, because Lisa didn't think they quite matched our living room décor.

I briefly considered taking them to work, but I don't really have the space for that… truth be told, I don't think they go with the décor in my office either. Maybe my wife has a point here? (Shh… don't tell her I said that.)

I should admit though, I do have a pretty impressive collection of caps—fifty-six in total. A shame I don't have enough heads to wear them all. Precisely why they now hang in my office.

My wife, Lisa, keeps a collection of purses in her closet, all of them nestled comfortably inside their dust covers. I've no clue why—she hasn't used most of them in years. I dare not touch or get rid of them... she knows *exactly* what's there. And I happen to enjoy being alive.

And baby clothes. Lisa has a few sealed storage bins, each one packed with the clothes our two kids wore when they were impossibly small—tiny shirts, even tinier socks, handfuls of fabric that once counted as outfits.

As I always do, I got curious and opened one of the boxes. I pulled out a onesie that made me stop and sit on the edge of a dusty bin, because suddenly I remembered holding an entire human being who somehow fit into something the size of a sandwich bag.

Damn. I got emotional.

Time really does sneak up on you while you're just trying to reorganize your stuff.

In another box, I found handwritten notes—the folded-up, middle-school love notes. Paper triangles and squares with "¿Do you like me?" scribbled in blue ink. Notes that meant more than grades, more than lunch money.

Notes that were basically the text messages of the '80s, except with better suspense and worse handwriting. Making those little notes and passing them around was both a specialized art and a covert mission.

My dad collects tools—why? Funny you should ask. Well, because, as he says, "you may need 'em someday." And boy, does he take that seriously. Multiple sets of every type of tool imaginable—more than any home handyman could dream of. Every hammer, every wrench, every gadget you can think of.

My mother's washroom has been completely overtaken by his tools, and that's not exactly a small space. Need 'em someday?

Well, that theory hasn't exactly panned out. He still has tools we gifted him years ago, still in their original packaging, waiting for a day that may never come.

My mom kept a collection of coffee cups. There were plenty in the kitchen cupboards for everyday use, but she also had a special set displayed on a rack in the dining room, just off the kitchen.

That collection was hers and only hers. Anyone who dared grab one of those cups risked losing a limb—okay, I'm kidding. But they would get the evil eye from her, and honestly, that was just as bad.

But her real love was her Tigers. She adored tigers. She had a robust collection of all things tiger-related: figurines, shirts, framed paintings—which, I may proudly say, included an original, life-size acrylic painting of a tiger's head rendered by yours truly. And I'm pretty proud of it—an amazing piece, if I do say so myself.

My sister Norma keeps a book about Boy George and Culture Club (damn—this goes waaay back). She even has a drawing she made of him, colored in with eyeshadow. It takes her back to her sophomore year in high school, when everything felt easier. She could be herself then. She didn't feel like she had to prove anything to anyone. She had great friends, great teachers. That music—and that moment—told her it was okay to be different.

Me? I've got a few collections of my own that I haven't laid a finger on in years. My MCU movies on Blu-ray, for instance—I don't even own a player anymore. Yet there they sit, proudly displayed on their own special shelf, glass doors and all, like relics in a tiny superhero museum. (They glare at me every time I walk by, silently judging my life choices.)

And the pièce de résistance—my Joe Montana trading card collection. My pride and joy. It took me years to assemble: well over 400 cards, meticulously sorted by year, all kept orderly in a heavy binder, with a handful in special hard cases. I store them in a sealed box, safe from dust, sunlight, and whatever else the world might throw at them.

Alongside the cards, I keep an assortment of Sports Illustrated magazines featuring Joe Cool. And, of course, the crown jewel of the collection—a 1981 near mint Joe Montana rookie card, sealed in hard acrylic. So far, it's the best specimen of his rookie card I've ever seen.

As a teacher—and now a school administrator—I was something of a collector. Remember that collection of caps I keep in my office?

Okay, let's be honest here: educators aren't collectors. They're hoarders. I already knew this—my wife was a teacher before I was, and I saw firsthand how much stuff she and her colleagues could amass.

I was no different. I followed her lead. Books, decorative borders, crayons, art supplies… the list goes on.

Remember that comment about staplers? Yeah… turns out it hit a little closer to home. My wife was a teacher. A third-grade teacher, to be exact—pretty much tailor-made to collect things. You know kids love to give gifts. And boy, did she have a collection.

Luckily for me, much of that stuff was generously left behind for the world to enjoy when she left her classroom. *But…* as it turns out, a healthy portion of her teacher supplies still resides in our garage.

I don't question it. Not anymore. I did once, and—well—all I remember is the lights going out and…

My own holdings have thinned out considerably since I left the classroom, and my offices have gotten smaller. Now, aside from the caps, I keep only a handful of trinkets and photos—just what I can pin to the corkboard next to my desk.

I keep a small collection of art books and comic trade paperbacks, and tucked among them—given more space than most—are not one but two collections of *Calvin and Hobbes*.

There's the heavy, reverent hardcover box set, the kind you lift with both hands, and the Portable Compendium, meant to be opened anywhere, anytime. I'm four volumes in on that one, with the fifth on its way, which feels oddly important, like finishing something I started decades ago without realizing it.

I know what it sounds like. It's just a comic strip, right? But it never was. *Calvin and Hobbes* was philosophy disguised as mischief, art hiding in the newspaper, a quiet agreement between creator and reader that imagination mattered and childhood wasn't something to rush through. It trusted kids to think deeply and adults to remember what they'd forgotten.

Maybe that's why it still sits there on my shelf, not as nostalgia alone but as a reminder—that small frames can hold big ideas, that humor can carry truth, that sometimes the most honest stories come with punchlines and a tiger who may or may not be real. In many ways, I saw myself in Calvin. Which, now that I think about it, is a little unsettling.

Rounding out my bookshelf are the yearbooks—one for each of my twenty-six years as an educator. Who knows? Maybe—just maybe—they'll have some stories to tell someday.

And—because of course—I have a 3D printer in my office. So naturally, scattered across my desk and windowsill are a few 3D-printed knickknacks, small modern artifacts added to an already well-documented life.

Standing there, looking at it all, thinking about it all, the absurdity finally hit me.

And I laughed.

I laughed because many of these things—these random, mismatched treasures—should've been thrown away years ago.

Yet somehow, they followed me through moves, phases, heartbreaks, paychecks, and new chapters.

Why? I'm not sure.

Maybe it's because that's what my parents did, and their parents before them.

Maybe it's just an unwritten, unspoken universal truth.

Maybe it's because these trinkets and artifacts remind me that I've lived a lot of life. I laughed, I loved, I messed up, I tried again, and somewhere along the way I tucked tiny souvenirs into boxes thinking, *I'll want this someday.*

Turns out… I did.

And as I sat there on the cold garage floor, surrounded by dusty memories and half-broken boxes, I realized something: I came out to declutter.

Instead, I ended up remembering.

And once again, the question comes up—why do we hold on to all this stuff?

Maybe because trinkets are proof. Proof that we lived, that we felt, that we loved dumb little things and big important people.

They're reminders that every phase of life—awkward, joyful, confusing, heartbreaking—left something behind worth holding.

They're tiny anchors, keeping us connected to who we were, who we are, and all the versions in between.

And maybe—just maybe—we keep them because one day, decades later, we'll pull them out of an old shoebox and finally understand just how much meaning a small, seemingly random object can carry.

Or we'll shrug, laugh, and wonder, *Why on earth did I keep this?*

Either way… we'll put it right back in the box. Just in case.

Like George Carlin said, "That's my stuff, and I gotta have it."

Only in my case, it isn't just stuff.

It's memory.

It's family.

It's proof that we were here, that we loved, that we laughed, and that we survived.
And maybe that's the only reason any of it matters at all.

Coming Home

Coming Home

Home is one of those words that carries weight far beyond its letters. It isn’t just a roof over your head or walls that have witnessed your childhood tantrums, homework disasters, and secret victories.

Home means many things to many people—and they’d all be right.

This won't be a story, so much as it is a reflection.

Home is a container for all the little versions of yourself you’ve ever been. It’s the smell of breakfast on a Sunday morning, the echo of laughter bouncing off familiar walls, the worn corner of a chair where someone always sat too long, thinking.

For some, home is a place.

A physical structure anchored to a specific address, with a roof that creaks in the heat and walls that know the sound of your footsteps. It’s the house you grew up in, or the one you’ve returned to, even if only in memory. You can still picture the way the light hit the living room floor in the late afternoon, or how the screen door slammed a little harder than it needed to.

For others, home is a feeling.

It’s comfort.

Safety.

Familiar noise.

It's knowing where everything is in the dark.

It's the smell of something cooking that doesn't need a recipe because it's been made the same way forever.

Home is the place where you don't have to explain yourself, where silence isn't awkward, and laughter comes easy.

Home can also be people. Sometimes it's not the building at all, but who's inside it. Parents. Siblings. Grandparents. Friends who showed up so often they practically had their own seat at the table. People who knew your routines, your moods, your stories—especially the ones you told over and over again, changing the details just enough to make them better each time.

And then there are those of us for whom home is memory. Not always perfect. Not always easy. But vivid. Sharp. Alive.

It's the place we carry with us long after we've moved on. The place that shows up unexpectedly—in a song on the radio, a random smell, or a quiet moment when the world slows down just enough to let the past tap us on the shoulder.

Even when you leave—college, a new job, another city—home follows you, tucked into the corners of your memory. It's in the smell of dust after rain, the creak of a screen door, the way sunlight hits the living room just so.

Coming back is never just about a place. It's about stepping into a living scrapbook of who you were, who you are, and the small, stubborn hope of who you might still become.

Home doesn't have to be ideal to be meaningful. It doesn't have to be permanent to be real. It just has to be yours.

And maybe that's the truest thing about home: we define it not by walls or addresses, but by the moments that linger—long after the door has closed behind us.

Home is a place defined not by walls, but by family, memory, and love—especially the presence of mom and dad…of familia.

My earliest memories are filled with Mom's warmth: waking to her singing, sharing café con leche and animal cookies with my dad, learning recipes at her side, and absorbing traditions through food, music, and daily routines.

The kitchen stood at the heart of our home, alive with the aromas of traditional dishes, the bustle of holiday preparations, and lessons passed down through generations.

Food and family gatherings define many of my strongest memories: carnes asadas, laughter, gossip, music, and celebrations carefully planned by Mom as expressions of love—and sometimes thrown together on the spur of the moment.

What might have started as a simple meal often turned into a full feast when family arrived unexpectedly: aunts, uncles, cousins—drinks, food, stories… memories in the making.

Family shaped my sense of belonging—chasing my brother and sharing playful moments with my sisters. My parents were steady anchors: my mom with her affection, discipline, and joy; my dad with his quiet presence, hard work, and small rituals tied to his city job. Somehow, his work carried over into our home, and though at the time we grumbled about chores (chores, ugh!), I now see they were quietly preparing me to take charge and stand on my own one day.

I remember a trip to Magic Mountain. Dad had just gotten off his shift at FedMart—it was late. Mom had a late dinner ready for him, and we, in our excitement, faked being asleep. Mom and dad packed us into the van and off we went to Valencia, my dad running on little to no sleep.

I don't remember much of the visit itself; the memories of the rides are vague. But I remember the drive: my siblings dozing in the back, my mom and dad singing and chatting, and me standing behind my dad in his captain's chair, asking questions about everything.

That night, the house, the sacrifices, and their quiet love all felt alive in the hum of the car and the laughter of a family together.

I remember the endless renovations made to the house—and the work they required. I remember how, when a project was finished, my dad would stand back and observe the completed work, beer in hand, a strange, satisfied smile on his face. I remember thinking it was odd that he did that. I didn't fully understand it until I had my own home and completed my own projects with my own hands. It was his way of demonstrating his love for us.

After moving away, home became even clearer in meaning. Not at first, but over time, I missed it deeply.

Home is not about homesickness; it is about gratitude—and the occasional guilt for not spending enough time together. It is comforting because it embodies unwavering love, forgiveness, and belonging.

Ultimately, home lives on through family, shared memories, and treasured photo albums that preserve the story of growing up together. My mom's house is a living museum of us. Every room is filled with photos and objects she collected over a lifetime—little representations of an evolving love and constant reminders of what was important to her.

A walk through any room in the house is a walk back through time, through childhood memories, recalling random moments known only to us—each of us carrying a slightly different take, often becoming the centerpiece of conversation at family gatherings.

My dad's man cave was his own little version of what my mom curated throughout the house. Newspaper clippings, photos of us, Pedro Infante, Vicente Fernández, Javier Solís, artwork made by my brother and me, a collection of tequilas (because what is Ranchera music without tequila?), and an impressive array of baseball caps. It was a place for him to be himself, but always surrounded by what he valued most—us.

After my mom's passing, home took on a new meaning.

Though it had changed, it had not diminished. Her presence still lingered, and a deeper connection with my dad emerged, revealing sides of him I or my siblings had not noticed before—his voice, his humor, his quiet ways of holding the family together.

The day she passed, we all returned home, drawn by the shared heartache that bound us. The house felt empty, almost hollow, yet her love remained—present, palpable, and quietly guiding us through the silence.

Home was the foundation that shaped my values, my ideas of marriage and parenting, and my lifelong sense of security.

Home was—and still is—Mom and Dad.

When I was growing up, my mom's kitchen always smelled like home. For me, her cooking was the bar by which all other foods were measured. After graduating and leaving for college, what I looked forward to most was her cooking. The aromas alone could make the miles shrink.

Her salsas in particular were heaven. The dry, smoky scent of chilitos toasting on the comal. The sweet tang of tomatoes blistering under the flame. The sharp, warm perfume of freshly crushed garlic, lingering like a promise. It was a smell that announced: something good is happening.

She made salsa like it was a ritual, grinding each ingredient slowly in her molcajete—a generations-old family treasure, pitted and smooth from decades of use. That tool was more than stone and mortar; it was a keeper of flavor and memory.

Even when you leave, home follows you.

For me, it followed in that molcajete, the taste of salsa on fresh tortillas, the crackle of chilitos on the comal, the curling perfume of garlic in the air.

A few years ago, my mom gave me a molcajete of my own. Handmade, rough-hewn, beautiful—a little piece of home. But it sat quietly on my shelf, waiting. Waiting for the moment I would finally honor it. And it felt like forever before that moment came.

One day, I finally seasoned it the way she had taught me and made my first salsa in it. The chilitos sizzled and crackled, the tomatoes blistered and popped, the garlic released its perfume. I ground them together slowly, letting the stone drink in the flavors.

When I tasted it, it wasn't just salsa. It was my mother's kitchen, my childhood, and now my own beginning with this new molcajete. Especially meaningful now that she is gone.

For Mexicanos, salsa is more than a condiment. It is tradition ground into stone. It is a language of the table, a way of saying, *this is home.* Salsa is the chorus of the meal, the unifying thread that brings together tortillas, beans, guisados, and rice. It carries the flavors of the earth—fire and heat, sweetness and salt, smoke and garlic—all pressed together in one small bowl.

We make salsa because it connects us to something larger than the kitchen. It is a ritual passed down through families, a moment of gathering before the meal begins. The grinding in the molcajete is a ceremony: it calls forth stories, recalls ancestors, preserves flavors. A bowl of salsa is not just taste—it is belonging. And in Mom's house, in her kitchen, it was love.

For me, this is home. It keeps me connected to my mom—and to all the memories of her: how she tended her plants, especially the chilitos; how she carefully gathered the ingredients for her salsas; and, of course, the rich, smoky smells that filled the house when she was toasting chilies and tomatoes, making the whole kitchen feel alive.

Making salsa the way she did in that molcajete is also a reminder that anything worth doing takes work—and when done with love, it makes anything we put it on that much better.

Home is messy.

It's loud.

It's your siblings shouting over each other like a tiny, chaotic stadium, your parents pretending not to notice the cookie you "borrowed," the dog demanding belly rubs as if no time has passed at all.

But that mess, that noise, that imperfect comfort—somehow, that is what home feels like. And in the kitchen, with salsa grinding in the molcajete, it is most alive. Salsa is memory made edible, a small yet enduring act of love.

It was visits to my nana's house in Mexicali, where the table was always full and the salsa always perfect.

It was early mornings at my grandma's, where the day began with huevos rancheros, beans, tortillas, and that familiar bowl of salsa.

It is the reason my cafecito tasted so good—because everything tasted better with her kitchen's warmth in it.

Coming home is never just about a place.

It's stepping into a living scrapbook of who you were, who you are, and the stubborn hope of who you might still become.

It is why we leave, and why, no matter how far we wander, we always long to return.

Afterward
INKBLOTZ

Afterword

As these stories come to a close, I keep thinking about the strange alchemy of memory—how a single afternoon, a fleeting joke, or a backyard misadventure can grow into a legend over the years.

Some of these tales are exactly as they happened; others have been "seasoned" by time, imagination, or the desire to make us look a little braver—or slightly more ridiculous—than we actually were.

But maybe that's the point of stories: to take the ordinary and make it sing, to spin the mundane into something that feels larger than life.

Writing this book was like walking down a street I half-remembered, half-dreamed. Cracked sidewalks. Murals peeling in the sun. Stray dogs that had long since wandered elsewhere.

All of it flickered between memory and myth. I could hear voices in the alleyways, see shadows of friends long gone, feel the echo of a neighborhood alive with mischief and possibility.

Some of these ghosts are still around; others exist only in these pages, and a few probably shake their heads whenever they see me coming with a notebook, muttering about "this one story."

In the borderlands where Calexico and Mexicali meet, the air itself seems to remember. The streets hum with stories that refuse to die: scraped knees and stolen snacks, audacious kids who believed a single afternoon could last forever, the way a ball bouncing down cracked asphalt became a kind of hymn.

Crossing into Mexicali was never just crossing a line—it was stepping into a different rhythm, a different gravity, a place where boldness and mischief gathered like smoke along the streets.

These pages hold sisters rolling their eyes at chaos, brothers doubling down on mischief, friends who mirrored our curiosity, and parents whose patience somehow survived the wild experiments of our youth.

They hold mornings chasing stray balls, afternoons spent haggling over arcade tokens, nights riding bikes as the horizon turned pink and orange, and days when the border felt like an invitation to something both impossible and inevitable.

Each story is a small echo of laughter, mistakes, and quiet lessons that shaped us—yet they feel bigger because of where we were.

To my siblings, my friends, my parents, and to my wife and kids—thank you for being part of this chaos, this music, this quiet magic. You didn't just live through these adventures—you made them unforgettable, weaving yourselves into the fabric of legend that now rests on these pages.

And to everyone reading this: may your own memories be as loud, as messy, as impossible, and as full of wonder as a small town at sunset, where the border bends and the air tastes of possibility.

Because in the end, it's not just the stories that matter—it's the people we share them with, the laughter that lingers long after the page is closed, and the way a single afternoon can stretch across decades like sunlight on a wall.

And if, while reading this, you find yourself remembering a scraped knee, a stolen snack, a game gone terribly wrong, or a friendship that somehow survived everything—good. That means you were paying attention. That means the legends worked.

The border—strange, stubborn, alive—is humming with stories, waiting for the next generation to step across it: a ball bouncing down cracked asphalt, a laugh carried on the wind, a small miracle waiting to be noticed.

ACKNOWLEDGMENTS

Acknowledgements

This second collection of stories took shape the same way most of my ideas do: slowly, unexpectedly, and usually at the worst possible time. Sometimes the words arrived while I was stuck in traffic.

Other times they showed up right when I was about to fall asleep—forcing me to get up, shuffle across the house like a confused zombie, and type before the idea evaporated. (If you ever heard random typing at 3 AM, that was me, not a burglar.)

Like anything we experience on this crazy rock floating in space, I believe these *legends* helped shape the person I am today.

There is a lot of history in these stories, a lot of love, and a whole lot of tiny moments that seemed insignificant back then but now feel like small miracles.

They are stitched together from the people who raised me, the friends who grew up alongside me, the border that shaped my world, and all the laughter, stubbornness, and chaos that came with it.

If these pages do anything, I hope they remind you—just as they reminded me—that the ordinary days of our past were never ordinary at all.

They were the beginning of who we would eventually become.

A huge thank you to my siblings—Harvey, Norma, and Aidee—for being *voluntary, involuntary, and occasionally unwilling* participants in the making of these stories. You starred in half of these memories without even knowing you were being cast, and the other half you've spent years pretending didn't happen.

Thank you for letting me retell our childhood "legends" with only mild exaggeration. (And Harvey, I promise—only *most* of it is true.)

To my dad, who always had stories to tell, lessons to give, and an endless supply of tinkering wisdom and *chicanadas* that somehow never got us arrested or grounded for too long. You taught me that anything could be fixed with a screwdriver, electrical tape, and enough confidence. Much of this book is basically your fault—so thank you.

To my mom, up in heaven—I know you would've helped tell these tales with twice the attitude, twice the heart, and at least three times the accuracy. I hope these pages make you smile. I miss you dearly, but I know you're with me as I relive these wonderful memories.

And every time a detail comes back sharper than expected, or a sudden laugh escapes me in the middle of writing, I feel you nudging me, reminding me not to forget the good stuff. Thank you for the stories you lived, the ones you passed down, and the ones I'm still discovering as I grow older. This book carries your fingerprints, even from heaven.

To my wife and kids—thanks for putting up with the creative spurts, the distracted "just one more paragraph" lies, and the moments when I drift off into Calexico flashbacks mid-conversation. Thank you for giving me the space to chase these stories, for nudging me back into the present when I disappear into the past, and for cheering every draft, every rewrite, and every weird idea I swear will "only take five minutes." This book exists because you let me dream loudly.

And finally, to that guy in the mirror—the only one who's been there from start to finish, whispering, "You might as well write it. Worst case, they laugh."

Turns out, he was right… *Again.*

About the Author

About the Author

Mariano Vélez grew up in Calexico, California, in the era of transistor radios, backyard baseball, and streetlight curfews—before video stores and cable TV became the center of every afternoon. The son of immigrants, he learned early the power of storytelling, the joy of laughter, and the magic that hides in the everyday.

Known as an Engineer of Learning, dad, husband, musician, cook, and perpetual tinkerer, Mariano has spent a lifetime collecting stories—some true, some remembered a little differently than they happened, and all told with a wink.

Shaped by life in two cultures—where the border between Mexico and the U.S. blurred—he grew up with mariachi in the air, tortillas on the stove, and adventures around every corner.

His writing captures the rhythm, flavor, and mischief of border life, where small-town streets become stages for impossible exploits, whispered rumors grow into legends, and the ordinary feels extraordinary.

An endless tinkerer and creator, Mariano spends his spare time making music, fixing things, doodling in quiet corners, and dreaming up new ways to tell old stories.

He currently serves as Dean of Students at Calexico High School, where he blends discipline with creativity, encouraging students to explore, build, perform, and imagine.

RUMORS, TALES, WHISPERS & WONDERS is his follow-up collection to *Mostly Made Up Stories from a Small Town Nobody*, inviting readers to wander back through the familiar streets of childhood, peek behind backyard fences, and discover the stories that linger long after the sun goes down—tall tales, quiet secrets, and every kind of mischief in between.

xinkblotz.com

www.ingramcontent.com/pod-product-compliance
Lightning Source LLC
LaVergne TN
LVHW010649110826
845149LV00014B/2997

9798994715109